Battle of the Artisans

Making the Bells of Marquis Yi

Irene Vinyard Bennett

Proverse Hong Kong

November 2023

BATTLE OF THE ARTISANS: MAKING THE BELLS OF MARQUIS YI tells the story of Tangtun, a conflicted, artistic twelve-year-old in 5th-century BCE China, who sets out to save his father from a killer. He crosses wits with his macho father and a vengeful king, armed thieves, and disgruntled villagers, and in the process, discovers new powers that rock his Bronze-Age world. In the end, what matters most is not Tangtun's artistic abilities or his father's muscles and might but that they realize the strength of acting together.

This novel portrays the making of the very real Bells of Marquis Yi, a 2500-year- old National Treasure of China. No one knows exactly why these bells were made, but Bennett provides a well-researched and persuasive solution to the mystery through her story of Tangtun and his village on the Yangtze River.

Every historical novel is an imagined introduction to a topic and a time. BATTLE OF THE ARTISANS invites readers to explore further the world and the science of the bells of Marquis Yi, to learn more about the early history of China, and to consider implications for the power of family and community. The author hopes that readers will connect with Tangtun and his world in ways that will enrich them and their own worlds.

From her first sharpened pencil to her latest computer, IRENE VINYARD BENNETT *BAU JI PING* loves writing. She bombards anything new with questions, researching and interviewing, until voila—a story is born! A native of Louisiana in south central USA, Irene earned her BA in English and Math, a master's degree in education, and did postgraduate studies in educational administration. A lover of words and numbers, culture, and history, this "people person" regales her family and friends with stories in real time, while writing curriculum and books, editing academic and theological writing, and teaching in America, Canada, Europe, and Asia. Irene spent a decade in Hong Kong teaching English to university students and multi-ethnic groups of women, and she traveled to Mainland China and a dozen Asian countries sharing educational methods with native teachers of English and religion. In every new place, Irene was learning while she taught. Irene now lives in Alexandria, Virginia, USA, with her husband, Phil, near her daughter, Malissa. She currently works in her nation's capital city, Washington DC, with the Western Presbyterian Church, as a next generation minister. Writing, public speaking, and teaching are still avid pursuits.

Battle of the Artisans Making the Bells of Marquis Yi

Irene Vinyard Bennett

Proverse Prize 2022

Lisa
Welcome to a Chinese family story
Irene

Proverse Hong Kong

Battle of the Artisans: Making the Bells of Marquis Yi
By Irene Vinyard Bennett
First published in paperback in Hong Kong
by Proverse Hong Kong,
under sole and exclusive right and licence,
21 November 2023.
ISBN-13: 978-988-8833-79-5
Alternate edition: ISBN 13: 978-988-8833-47-4
Ebook edition: ISBN-13: 978-988-8833-48-1

Distribution (Hong Kong and worldwide)
The Chinese University of Hong Kong Press,
The Chinese University of Hong Kong,
Shatin, New Territories, Hong Kong SAR.
E: cup@cuhk.edu.hk; W: https://www.cup.cuhk.edu.hk
Proverse page: https://cup.cuhk.edu.hk/Proversehk
Distribution (United Kingdom)
Stephen Inman, Worcester, UK.
Enquiries to Proverse Hong Kong
P.O. Box 259, Tung Chung Post Office,
Lantau, NT, Hong Kong SAR, China.
E: info@proversepublishing.com
W: https://www.proversepublishing.com

Illustrations and cover image by Paulette Ferguson,
Cover design by Artist Hong Kong.

British Library Cataloguing in Publication Data
A catalogue record for the first paperback edition
is available from the British Library

DEDICATION

To teachers of music, history, science, and language arts, who influence and inspire young artists: and in memory of three such teachers of mine: James Shannon, Helen Shannon, and Lucien E. Coleman, Jr.

* * *

The real voyage of discovery consists not in seeking new landscapes but in having new eyes.
—Marcel Proust (1871-1922)

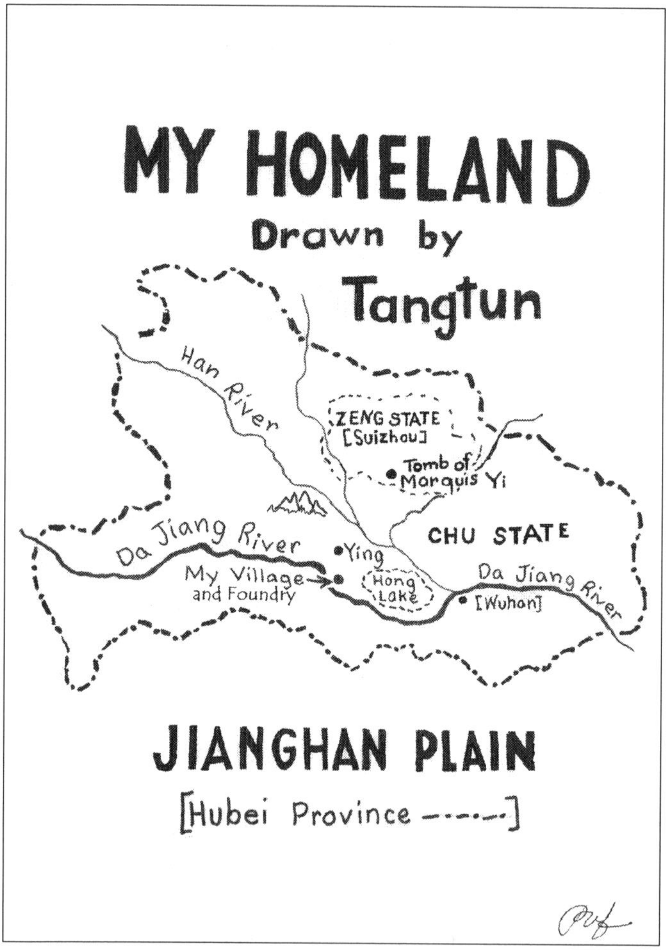

Ancient China
Along the Yangtze River
456 BCE

TABLE OF CONTENTS

Acknowledgements	9
Chapter 1	11
Chapter 2	16
Chapter 3	24
Chapter 4	28
Chapter 5	33
Chapter 6	39
Chapter 7	42
Chapter 8	46
Chapter 9	51
Chapter 10	54
Chapter 11	59
Chapter 12	63
Chapter 13	66
Chapter 14	69
Chapter 15	73
Chapter 16	77
Chapter 17	83
Chapter 18	87
Chapter 19	90
Chapter 20	94
Chapter 21	99
Chapter 22	104
Chapter 23	109
Chapter 24	114
Chapter 25	118
Chapter 26	121
Chapter 27	125
Chapter 28	128
Chapter 29	131
Chapter 30	135
Chapter 31	141
Chapter 32	146
Chapter 33	150
Chapter 34	155
Chapter 35	158
Chapter 36	162

Chapter 37	166
Chapter 38	168
Chapter 39	171
Chapter 40	175
Chapter 41	180
Chapter 42	184
Chapter 43	189
The time of Tangtun	197
The bells today	198
Facts about the bell set	200
Author's note	203
Advance comments	207

TABLE OF ILLUSTRATIONS

by Paulette Ferguson

Ancient China. Along the Yangtze River, 456 BCE	6
Tangtun Runs Away	11
Men do what men have to do	46
A good father makes a clever son	59
Kill that traitor!	77
Who is your father?	104
How can I make it up to them?	125
Can we count on you?	135
Together we win!	158
We. Are. Dead.	175
When music goes forth…	189

ACKNOWLEDGEMENTS

Telling a new story starts with an idea, advances with imagination, research, starts-stops-detours-reverses, and then becomes a finished tale with the help of critiques from informed readers. To all such helpers who contributed to the creation of BATTLE OF THE ARTISANS, I express my profound gratitude.

The first draft was completed via the marvelous NaNoWriMo online tool after Johnathan Leung, a nine-year-old Hong Konger read the first three chapters and asked for the rest of the story.

My author teachers at the Institute of Children's Literature, Terri Martin and Jan Fields, encouraged me to submit my first chapter and outline to publishers.

Chinese friends provided invaluable language translation and cultural critiques throughout the process. For their generous and unique expertise, I thank Victor Lin Chao, a native of the Wuhan area, Yidi Tsao, Michelle Zhou, Jessica Zhang, and Ya Gao. Most important were the cultural explanations and language assistance I received from my Cantonese teacher, Johnny Lee.

Members and critique groups of the Society of Children's Book Writers and Illustrators (SCBWI) Hong Kong walked alongside me as they read parts of the story and responded with constructive ideas. In the process they became creative partners who share responsibility for this story, though not any final shortcomings. With a grateful heart, I name first Mio Debnam, who always thought more of my work than I did; Jan Fields who would not let me give up on this story; and countless others, namely, Dorcas Cheng-Tozun, Darien Tso, Susan Eitemiller (now, sadly, no longer with us), John Brennan, Elizabeth Grobler, Jane Houng, Kathleen Ahrens, Bhakti Mathur, Ritu Hemnani, Rick Beasley, Virginie L. Zurcher, Larry Baum, Rachel Ip, Dora Tsang.

A professional artist, my sister Paulette Vinyard Ferguson, retold the story through beautiful pen and brush strokes. Her gifted contribution to our readers is invaluable.

The final version of this story reflects the professional shaping by the Proverse Publishing team, especially Gillian and Verner Bickley. Thank you for your patient and persistent work.

Finally, in the spirit of this story, I recognize with humble appreciation the cocoon of family support in which I worked. Phil Bennett, my life partner, and Malissa Bennett, my daughter, provided uninterrupted cheering on!

I also thank the judges of the Proverse Prize 2022 for recommending that I be a winner for that year.

CHAPTER 1

Tangtun runs away

"He'll kill you!"

Lin's fierce words pierced the predawn silence like the gong at the village gate.

What? Tangtun froze on the window-sill with head and shoulders outside their mud-brick house and his right leg dangling inside. He strained to make sense of the low voices coming from just beyond the curtain that separated his tiny sleep corner from the rest of the family,

His dad said, "I won't let him kill me, Lin. I have a plan."

A killer! thought Tangtun. He dropped down from the window, eased his roll of clothes and art supplies off his shoulder, and inched along the packed-dirt floor toward a sliver of light edging the curtain.

"You've avoided him for years. Why risk your life now?" Lin said.

Squinting through the crack, Tangtun could see his parents on the opposite wall of the one-room home. The oily smoke from the clay lamp beside the earthen bed pricked his eyes as the flickering light reflected off his mother's tear-streaked face. She sat on the edge of the bed in her gray tunic gripping the arms of his bare-chested father who towered over her like a stone statue.

Studying them, Tangtun noted the play of lamplight across his father's bulging muscles and wished this stern man would be his gentle giant of a dad again like he used to be. He shook off the memory and held his breath.

Jianjun said, "Our work can save us. Our work will save us."

"He believes you betrayed him." Her words sped up. "And, he beheads people!"

"I can protect myself," he interrupted her.

"But, think of our family."

"I've got no choice. I must do this, or none of us will survive."

The tree-bark sound of his voice scraped down Tangtun's spine so hard he winced and shivered.

Lin shook his arms, "I beg you. Don't."

He bent down and spat words in her face like water popping on hot metal, "Sky God rewards men who work hard!"

Lin threw her hands up like a shield and Tangtun lurched back. He tripped over his go-roll and grabbed at the thin curtain, bringing it down with him. Scooting away like a crab, he couldn't dodge his father's swinging hand.

Swa-a-at!

"*Ai-yah!*" Tangtun held his hurting cheek and glared.

"Go back to sleep, now," Jianjun ordered.

"A killer, BaBa? Who is it?"

"Quiet! Adult concerns aren't yours!"

With face burning and nostrils flaring, Tangtun clenched his teeth, jutted out his chin, and watched Ba slap the curtain back into place.

A killer not my concern? Hitting me just for asking? Well, see if I care!

He grabbed up his roll of belongings, tossed it out the window, and scrambled after it. Wind-blown tree branch fingers pointed toward a path of freedom through the shadowy village.

Creeping around his grandmother's room added on to the rear of the house, he slid as quiet as one of his paint brushes to the front, jumped the drainage ditch, and stomped down the dirt lane to his best friend's house, a match for all twenty, thatch-roofed houses of the village. He leaned in the window.

"*Psst,*" he whispered. Silence.

"Hey," he said a little louder.

Across the room, Big Ming mumbled in his sleep. Just then Little Ming, only a warm lump in the darkness, slid past Tangtun and dropped to the ground grunting, "Ready."

"Let's go," Tangtun took off along the lane ahead of his constant companion.

"What's the big hurry?"

"Need to get away before anyone sees us."

They pounded side by side through the early morning mist, passed through the village gate, and headed up the rocky road away from Da Jiang, the Great River. Their hard breathing poked holes in the blanket of river fog covering them.

Tangtun couldn't stop fuming about his "new" Ba. *I have to get away from him.* But, he couldn't quit thinking about MaMa's words either. *Who's a killer? Why?*

"Little Ming, we have a problem."

"What problem? Your Ba slapping you around again?"

"Worse than that. Somebody might try to kill him."

"What?" Little Ming stopped still in the middle of the road and grinned. "You mean besides you?"

Tangtun knew he was teasing, but he couldn't laugh. He lifted one shoulder and chewed his lip. *We've always done everything together, never kept secrets, but should I talk to him about this new family problem?*

"Never mind, we need to find that army camp."

"Wait. A killer? Who?"

"I don't know. I just heard about it. That's all."

Little Ming shook his head. "I haven't." After a few steps, he said, "Wait! If there's a killer loose in our village, why are we leaving?

"What can we do?"

"Fight, that's what!"

"Fight? Ha! We're the smallest of all the foundry apprentices. The army won't take us as soldiers, but they just might let us be kite spies."

They ran on up the tree-lined road without speaking for a few minutes. Then Little Ming said, "Master Musician took another kite he made to the soldiers' camp last week. He can help us."

Picturing the round, wrinkle-free face of the village elder, who never frowned or fussed, and surely wasn't the killer, Tangtun nodded. "Right, the Master knows everything."

He picked up his anger-fuelled, get-away pace.

CHAPTER 2

The boys charged uphill toward narrow Elbow Pass, the last challenge for travelers before the road topped the bluff to cross the level plain to the capitol city of Ying. Just before the tricky pass, Tangtun turned left on a path leading to the Master Musician's place.

He breathed a deep breath and relaxed a little, saying, "We're safe. No one is likely to pay any attention to us this far from the village."

Then he stepped off the path into the trees, stood with legs spread to relieve himself through his open-crotched pants, and stared up at the dripping branches. Overhead the Great Bear's tail pointed the direction geese would fly ahead of wintry winds. Just thinking of the graceful birds made his fingers itch to draw. *Without Ba to fuss at me for wasting time*, he thought, *I can sketch boulders and late summer flowers along the road. I sure won't miss his fussing.*

He felt for the lump of charcoal he kept in his waist pouch with his knife and found an empty space. He said to his friend, "*Ai-yah*, no knife. If Ba finds out, he'll yell and say I lost it."

"No need to worry about him anymore," Little Ming said, starting along the path again.

A chill spread through Tangtun at his words, as if the wintry wind had arrived early. He shivered and said, "I'm not. No killer will get the best of him, I'm sure. Besides," he mimicked his dad's voice, "'Adult business is no concern of mine.'"

Near another small, thatch-roofed house nestled alone in a grove of ghost trees above the village, Tangtun smelled the nutty fragrance of rice cooking and heard talking and laughter. He stopped. "Master has a visitor. Let's keep going."

But, the village elder spotted them and stood up from his morning rice bowl. His tall, robed body filled the open door. "Good morning, boys. Have you eaten breakfast yet?"

"No, Master," they chorused together.

Little Ming laughed and pushed Tangtun's shoulder in fun. Tangtun just frowned.

"Come in and meet my friend, visiting from the state of Wey."

As they stepped inside, the Master turned toward a short man with bushy eyebrows and a gray beard falling across his chest. "Zigong, these are the boys of whom I spoke earlier. This is Tangtun and this, Little Ming."

The boys automatically bowed their heads toward the man seated at the small table.

"You boys going fishing before work?" asked Master Musician.

"We only came to ask a question," said Tangtun, rocking from one foot to the other, eager to go before anyone came looking for them. The elder raised his eyebrows and waited.

"First, sit a moment," said Zigong, pulling his long robe close to his leather-clad feet and gesturing with an open hand at the floor near his low wooden stool. Both boys knew to respect their elders, so they pushed their rolls behind the small chime stone rack near the door and obeyed. "You both have long hair, wear identical gray pants and tunics, and hemp shoes. Are you twins?"

The boys grinned at each other. "No, just best friends," said Tangtun.

"The Master tells me you two think a lot about everything. Tell me where you want to go in life."

Immediately in one breath Little Ming waved his arms and tapped his toes and said, "Where I can dance and sing and have fun! And do it with Tangtun, of course!"

The men laughed and nodded at each other while Tangtun wondered how to speed up the talk, so they could get back on the road before their fathers realized they were gone. He accepted the bowl of steaming congee topped with bits of fish from Master and gulped it down, burning his mouth in the process. He blew *hoohoohoo* to cool it while Little Ming laughed out loud.

When Zigong only waited patiently, Tangtun gave up on hurrying the elders and spoke. "I love colours, drawing, cutting and shaping things with my hands." He motioned with his chopsticks and then dropped his hands. "But, Ba wants me to learn metal work and sword fighting."

"Who is your father?" Zigong leaned toward Tangtun.

"Jianjun. He runs the foundry."

"Are you like him?"

He shook his head. "He's big and strong, not afraid of anything. I'm little, but I can lift Little Ming off the ground and toss him, so I'm strong."

He frowned and continued, "But, I think all the time and have ideas, too."

Little Ming said, "Right! He daydreams all the time."

"So Ba says." Tangtun nodded. Then he lowered his head to hide his face and spoke low words at his knees. "Should I want to be like him instead?"

"We all learn to do the needed things of life, young Tangtun," said Zigong. "And having questions may be the most needed of all. Life answers boys who question it."

Reminded of the reason for their visit, Tangtun said, "My question now is, where can we find the king's army?"

Master Musician said, "North of the capital city, a good day's waggon ride up the main road. Didn't you ask your father?"

When Tangtun only shrugged and gobbled his rice faster, the Master Musician turned to his friend and said, "Fathers. My father called me lazy when I blew tunes on my bamboo flute instead of working. I became quite angry, of course." He chuckled and continued, "But later when other people wanted to hear me play the same *dizi* as well as the chime stones and bell set, he accepted my being a musician."

Tangtun stared into his rice bowl, certain his father would never accept his being an artist, but he stayed quiet, again out of respect for his elders.

"Fathers and sons," Zigong slapped his knee, "an age-old problem. Earlier we were talking about loyalty. Did I tell you the governor of She District once asked my teacher, Kongzi, about something that happened there between a father and son?"

The musician shook his head no.

"The governor told us of a man named Upright Gong. When his father stole a sheep and was caught, Upright Gong testified against him. The governor wanted to know Kongzi's opinion of the son."

Tangtun asked, "Sir, what did your teacher say?"

"He said, 'In my native place, upright people are quite different from that son.'"

Zigong put his hand on his chest and quoted his teacher further. "'To us, an upright father covers up his son's misdeeds and an upright son covers up his father's wrongdoing.'"

Tangtun tipped his head sideways. "Really? I wonder ..."

"You wonder?"

Knowing he shouldn't talk to a stranger about family matters but hoping he could understand better, he risked telling them. "Ba gets mad at me about everything these days. He hates my artwork, my fly-away hair, and wants me to be a man like him." He sighed while the older men waited. He finished in a rush. "Maybe being an army kite spy is better."

"*Hmm*, a kite spy," The Master looked him up and down. "You could be. You're the right size."

"And then everything would be well?" Zigong asked.

Tangtun's nails bit into the palms of his fisted hands as he decided to reveal his big, family secret. "No, it wouldn't be! Someone wants to kill my Ba. What can I do?"

With raised eyebrows, the village elder leaned forward. "How do you know this?"

"I heard MaMa and BaBa talking."

"Perhaps you misunderstood them?"

"I don't think so."

"Whatever you heard," Zigong held his hands vertically together in front of him and moved them in time with his words. "By nature, fathers and sons have more love for each other than anyone else. It's the way of life, Tangtun."

Wide-eyed and shaking his head, Tangtun sputtered. "But BaBa hits me!" He looked over at his friend. "He didn't use to do that, did he, Little Ming?"

"No, he didn't."

Tangtun pursed his lips and said, "But now, hmm. I wonder. What if BaBa did something, like hit somebody hard, injured him, and now that person intends to kill him?"

Zigong stroked his beard and was quiet for so long, Tangtun squirmed, thinking, I've done it now—made another mistake—talked when I shouldn't. The aching spot on his shoulder, where Ba had hit him yesterday for dropping wood in the cauldron of hot metal at the foundry, reminded him of Ba's strange reactions to his mistakes.

"Maybe something, maybe nothing, we don't know," said Zigong. "So, have patience, young man. Sometimes wisdom comes from bitter experience."

"Waiting's hard, Honorable Teacher, 'cause I have many questions."

The Master Musician stood up. "Indeed your Ba may have concerns you don't know about, Tangtun. Think about it. Now, weren't you boys going somewhere?"

"Yes, thank you, Master, for the breakfast, and thank you, Sir Zigong, for talking with us."

The boys bowed, picked up their rolls and stepped outside.

Walking away, Tangtun reran over and over in his mind Master Zigong's story of the son testifying against his father. At the road, he stopped with his bundle on his shoulder and his fidgeting friend beside him. He looked left toward the distant capital city of Ying and then downhill to his right toward Jingnan Village.

Feeling like a tightly stretched bow, he stepped toward the city and then reversed himself and walked toward the village. His loose hair brushed over one shoulder and then the other as he switched directions again and again between the freedom of the army and problems at home.

The woods around him woke up. Birds sailed smoothly overhead, and a mother deer and her fawn strolled across the dusty road. A lizard scooted toward his foot and then detoured in a lightening zigzag under a bush.

"Everybody knows which way to go except me," he said through clamped teeth.

"Let's play Hand Command to choose," said Little Ming, shaping his hand and fingers quickly through the symbols for poisonous centipede, frog, and snake.

"Be serious for once, won't you?"

“C’m o-o-on. If you win, we look for the army. If I win, we go home.”

“Unh-uh. That’s a little boys’ game. It can’t decide this for me."

Zigong’s statement echoed in his mind, “Sons cover up for fathers’ wrongdoing.”

Tangtun stopped pacing and gripped Little Ming’s shoulder, “I don’t know why BaBa is being so mean to me, but if someone wants to kill him, I can’t run away to be a kite spy. I must help him even if he did something wrong.”

Without another word, he turned his face toward home—and an unknown killer. His faithful friend followed.

CHAPTER 3

Back at the house, Tangtun hid his clothes under a basket in the empty yard to sneak inside later. He stiffened when his little sister Meimei came out the door with their father, but for once she asked no questions while slipping a cucumber into Tangtun's hand.

"Where were you?" asked Ba. "Drawing birds again?"

"In the woods with Little Ming," said Tangtun, starting off toward work before his dad could ask more questions.

Just beyond the village gate, a company of battle-ready soldiers stood in formation in the road, listening to their commander bark orders. Red-and-black painted leather helmets matched their mid-thigh body armour. Each held a bronze-tipped, bamboo spear upright at his side. Munching on the cucumber, Tangtun asked, "What's happening, Ba?"

"They're marching downriver to conquer more people of the Jianghan Plain. King Wang fights when he doesn't have to." Ba cleared his throat of morning crud and spat on the ground. "He's a greedy man."

"Sure are a lot of them," said Tangtun.

"This? It's only part of the King of Chu's army. The archers passed by the village about daylight."

Tangtun thought, *Little Ming and I probably just missed them on our way home.*

Ba continued. "More swordsmen on horses won't be far behind these."

As the company marched away, he looked directly at Tangtun. "You can join them one day," he said in his don't-argue-with-me voice. "You should stop all that drawing and painting and master the sword. Then when our people need protecting, you can fight beside your brothers. Remember, *du li nan zhi*. One person alone is not strong enough."

"But I like doing things by myself," Tangtun said.

Ba grunted, "*Huh!*"

Tangtun quickly changed the subject. "How do you know so much about the army anyway?"

"My name, Jianjun, means Builder of Armies," His face tightened and his fingers curled, "for all that matters now."

Now how did I irritate him, wondered Tangtun, but he forged ahead, "So, why are you a metal worker and not a soldier?"

"The king's army cannot fight without the weapons we make!" Ba punctuated his words with a hatchet-like hand.

Seeing his dad didn't really answer his question, Tangtun switched tactics. "I know we make spearheads, arrow tips, axes, and even chariot axle blades for them."

"Yes, and other foundries do, too."

Just then a company of soldiers with sheathed swords on their hips pounded toward them on lean horses. Tangtun gasped when the captain saluted his father and said, "You're good, Jianjun!"

Jianjun tipped his head.

"You know him, Ba?"

"We worked together before you were born."

Watching the swordsmen ride on by, Tangtun scrunched his eyes, licked the dust from his lips and asked, "In the army? Were you a swordsman, Ba?"

Ba ignored him. "See the swords they are wearing? We made most of those, but now, there's a new metal called iron. Soon other foundries will start making a lot of swords of that, and I'm worried the army won't need our bronze ones anymore."

"Really? What's so special about iron, Ba?"

"Everyone hopes it will make sharper, stronger swords," Ba trudged on. "If it can do that, it'll run us out of business."

"Then, let's make iron swords," Tangtun said slapping a fist in his hand.

"We don't know ironwork. The first foundry around here to make iron swords will work for the king. He will no longer need bronzework, and our whole village will suffer."

The bitter sound of his voice made Tangtun scrunch his eyes and mouth like his cucumber had suddenly changed into a sharp-tasting ginger root.

"Surely we can do something," said Tangtun.

"For now we keep working. Hard times cannot be avoided." Ba walked with his shoulders slumped, his hands clasped behind his back, and his head dropped.

"Can you do another job, Ba?"

"I'll find something, but it won't be easy. King Wang may interfere if he discovers where I am."

"Why?" Tangtun said.

Ba lifted his head and scowled. "His anger rules his life now."

"How do you know that, Ba?"

"When we were young, our families were friends," Ba stared with a still face into the distance beyond the riders' dust cloud, "friends, a long time ago."

"Really? Now if he finds you, what will happen?"

"Stop asking questions! The young don't need to know everything." Ba slapped Tangtun's shoulder and pushed him down the road. Tangtun stumbled forward and then began to drag his feet in the dirt, slowing down deliberately to annoy his father.

"Faster," said Ba pushing him again. "We must work harder to survive."

Tangtun stretched his stride to match Ba's long steps, but he shook a mental fist at Ba and his ghost killer. Like a thunderstorm growing in the afternoon sky, angry darkness lurked along the edges of his mind and spread across his face. He saw Zigong again in his mind and asked himself, a good son protects this kind of father? He glared ahead and vowed to find the killer himself. Maybe that would change things.

CHAPTER 4

Turning down the rocky bluff path to Da Jiang, the Great River, Tangtun studied fishing boats already tied up at water's edge with the sun twinkling in rainbow colours off the scaly morning catch. *I have to draw that picture soon*, he thought.

The foundry was in constant motion, busy like it had been ever since his mother's grandfather started it. Wooden carts with horses straining under their heavy weight rumbled along the pock-marked road below. Apprentices helped drivers unload ingots of copper and tin and pile them inside the gate and waved goodbye to them as they turned their empty carts back toward the mines in the distant, western mountains. Men's yells carried over the bangs of hammers and scraping metal in the weathered, wooden workshops lining the river's edge.

Smoke from the clay furnaces burned Tangtun's nose as he entered. His spit had a metallic taste. He picked up a stray, rust-coloured stone and traced its brown and green veins. "Looks like an old man with a beard, like the Master Musician," he murmured to himself. "I wonder if I polish it…"

"Better stop daydreaming, Tangtun," Little Ming almost sang his words.

Tangtun looked up. His best friend's bare feet danced in quick patterns while his stringy arms balanced a wheelbarrow of coal. Some pieces bounced off and rolled with it down toward the alloys. True to his happy name, Little Ming brightened the day just as he always had.

Tangtun called back, "You'd like this daydream, Little Ming."

His steps slowed near the alloy furnace, the place of his earlier humiliation. The wood he had dropped in the hot pot had sunk before he could move, like a giant dragon gulped it and belched dirty streaks in the liquid bronze, as pink as the river salmon he loved to eat. Heat from the furnaces made him sweat, and his arm muscles quivered like they too remembered his father's punishing whack for adding more scum to the liquid bronze.

"Move along, Tangtun," an older apprentice bellowed from underneath his load of dross, "before you make another dumb mistake!"

"*Ai-yah*!" Tangtun almost backed into the firepit with its bubbling cauldron in the middle. He looked around, ready for jokes and jeers for his clumsiness, but no one noticed.

Imitating the sliding voice of the other boy, he yelled back, "You're the mis-ta-aa-KE maker, Haohao." He used the apprentices' special name for him, his name Hao plus the sound-alike word hao that meant good—because he wasn't.

Little Ming's laugh and Haohao's scowl made Tangtun fearless. He moved closer to Haohao and said, "Did you take my knife? Planning to kill someone with it?"

"What? No, never! You lost it more likely."

"I wouldn't lose it. Ba made it for me." Tangtun blinked at the pride ringing in his own voice.

"You don't hunt, so nothing to skin. You just carve toy animals for your little sister."

Tangtun stepped even closer, almost chest to chest, and said, "I will get it back." For a minute, Haohao glared back, but then he turned away. Tangtun wondered if the bigger and newest apprentice might be the killer. Had Haohao taken his knife to attack his father?

At the smith shop, Tangtun greeted with respect the burly coppersmith, Red. "Had breakfast yet?"

Red rubbed a tin-edged sword at an angle in a repeating wave across a smoothing stone anchored on a big tree block worn down by years of use. His motion was mesmerizing as he sharpened the sword so sharp it would cut through leather in one swipe.

Tangtun spoke louder. "Is that blade ready for an apprentice to try?"

Wiping his sweat out of his eyes, Red laughed his deep-throated laugh and said, "I've eaten, Tangtun, but you'll need a few more bowls of rice to grow tall enough to swing this sword."

"I'm short, but I guess I could learn if I have to."

He ran his hand along the carved handle of a finished blade, wondered if this smiling man could harbour killing thoughts, and asked, "Were you ever a soldier?"

"Who, me? Nah. I've always been a coppersmith."

"BaBa has a sword behind his workbench."

"Your father doesn't talk about that sword, Tangtun. It reminds him of a bad time long ago." Nodding his head and arching his eyebrows toward the outside, he said, "Here he comes. Ask him about it yourself."

Before Tangtun could move on, Ba gripped his shoulder so hard he winced. "Visiting instead of working again? Ask me what?"

Through gritted teeth, Tangtun said, "About the sword behind your workbench,"

"Good! You saw my sword," said his father. "It's time I taught you to fight, Tangtun."

"I like art, BaBa, not fighting," Tangtun said, but then thought, *With a killer around I'd better learn.*

Ba's long braid swung as he shook his head. "Sooner or later, everybody has to fight. We'll start practicing tonight after work. Now, stop dallying, and go help Little Ming unload that coal. We must keep a hot fire going to melt the copper."

Jumping to obey, Tangtun overheard Ba tell Red, "Important lunch time today. Spread the word to all the men," and wondered, *Now what's that about? The killer maybe?*

All morning Tangtun tramped around following orders to "Go get this" and "Carry that"—dirty, sweaty apprentice work. Even watching the wax disappear in the "lost wax" casting of an ornamental bowl didn't interest him like it did other days. Angry thoughts about Ba roiled together in his head—*What did you do? Hit the wrong person?* Every time a worker told him to do something, he looked for menace in his face or voice.

Then he bumped against Haohao who pushed him so hard his buckets of dross swayed and threw him off-balance. "*Ai-yah*!" he yelled as his feet crossed and one bucket dumped dross on to the ground. He leaned the opposite way and the other bucket slid off the end of the shoulder rod, banging on the ground and scattering dross bits in every direction.

"Shovel it up, Tangtun," his father ordered while Haohao laughed.

Glaring at Haohao, Tangtun scraped up dross and growled. "I have bigger things to think about than you, Haohao."

Then he thought again, *Big, mean Haohao. I bet you are the killer!*

"Did you know Ba before you moved here?"

Haohao stared with his mouth open and gulped. "Of course not. I didn't know anyone in Jingnan village except my uncle. Why?"

"Never mind," Tangtun said and thought, *BaBa doesn't avoid you like MaMa said he avoids the killer. So, if it's not you, who is it? And how will I ever find him?*

CHAPTER 5

At the sound of the noontime gong, Tangtun and Little Ming jogged along the grassy bank of the Great River. They headed toward the workers' usual hillside lunch spot above the foundry.

Tangtun said, "BaBa's teaching me the sword, starting tonight."

"Can I learn, too?" asked Little Ming.

"Probably. I don't care about fighting, but we need to know how—just in case."

"In case what?" said Little Ming.

"If something bad happens..."

Just then two hands landed squarely on Tangtun's back and shoved him, splashing into the river. He grabbed a willow branch to keep from being pulled out into the swift current. Thrashing around, he got his footing, and then he clambered up the bank and took off after the snickering boys running up the hill.

"Who pushed me? I'll get you," he yelled swiping wet hair out of his eyes without slowing down.

Everyone just kept running and laughing except Little Ming who kept stride with him. "It was old Haohao."

They arrived on the hilltop just behind the older boys. "You swim like a rock, Tangtun," taunted Haohao, hitching up his pants that always seemed on the verge of falling off.

Tangtun stuck his face up with his chin almost on Haohao's chest and glared into the taller boy's face. "Careful, Haohao, a rock can do a lot of damage." He turned to follow Little Ming to a seat.

The canopy of a jade lily tree with fading blooms shaded the workers from the late summer sun. Like family, everyone shared simple food—pieces of cold fish, soup and sticky rice.

"Your fish is so black today," Little Ming teased the mold maker.

"Hmm, maybe because my wife cooked it in the da-a-ark of ni-i-ght?" He stuck his face close to Little Ming's and made loud ghost noises. When Little Ming jumped, he slapped his knee and roared with laughter.

Usually Tangtun joined in the fun, but today he leaned silently in wet clothes on a knotty tree root. He pulled his damp coal from his waist pouch and laid it in the sun to dry.

"What's with old Haohao?" he asked Little Ming.

Little Ming shrugged. "Don't know."

"Nobody acts like him."

"Right, 'cause he's not really one of us maybe?"

Just then Ba stood up in front of the workers to speak. "Men, you know King Wang wins every battle he fights."

"And always takes more land," said one man to Ba's right.

"And makes Chu slaves of the enemies he doesn't kill," said another.

The mold maker rounded out their views with, "I think he enjoys killing more than fighting!"

From the back of the crowd, the boys shoved and slapped at each other. Haohao said, “Right, wins every time. He’s a mighty king!”

Tangtun mumbled to Little Ming, “Sounds like a murdering monster to me.”

Little Ming lifted his eyebrows high and opened his eyes and mouth wide. “Oo-ooo.” Worrying about a killer closer to home, Tangtun couldn’t laugh at him.

Ba added, “When he dies, other kings can say, ‘No horror remains to scare us,’ and they’ll be right.” Murmurs of agreement went through the crowd.

Tangtun’s eyes nearly popped out of his head, and he grabbed Little Ming’s arm. “Maybe it’s the king who wants to kill Ba,” he whispered.

Little Ming lifted his eyebrows and tightened down his lower lip. “No way! Why would he be? He doesn’t even know your dad.”

“Yes, he does.” Little Ming’s eyebrows raised even higher and his eyes widened. Tangtun said, “I’ll explain later.”

They stared at each other with jaws dropped as Ba continued speaking, “This time he took a small kingdom without shedding a drop of blood.”

“Unbelievable!”

Tangtun stretched up to see who spoke. The caster sprawled on the grass had *Impossible* written all over his craggy face. Tangtun thought, *He’s so disagreeable, he could be a killer, couldn’t he? No, the king is more likely.*

"It's simple. King Wang's son saw the beautiful sister of the Zeng ruler. So, instead of war, a royal wedding is planned," said Ba.

"Girl gets boy again," laughed Haohao elbowing the apprentice next to him. Other boys mimicked him. Tangtun's father's mouth turned up at the boys' antics.

Tangtun pushed his lips tight together and puffed through his nose, like an angry bull. Resentment ran through his mind. Not funny, Ba. You smile at their foolishness but hit me. He kicked at the tree root.

"King Wang's father became friends of the Zeng when we lost the Battle of Ying decades ago," a worker observed.

"A terrible battle indeed," said Tangtun's father nodding.

A couple of the apprentices said, "What happened? Tell us!"

"During that battle, our Chu capitol fell and King Wang's father escaped to the home of the Zeng people. Later that friendly ruler helped him get the city back. When those two died, their sons, King Wang and Marquis Yi, came to power, and until now, they have not been friends at all."

Tangtun watched Ba breathe deeply, shake his head as if ridding himself of bad memories, and continue. "I've just learned good news today. King Wang has declared a different kind of battle, a Battle of Artisans, to create the perfect wedding gift for Marquis Yi of Zeng. And the winning foundry will become a royal founder of the king and its leader, the Royal Artisan of the Chu."

Tangtun asked, "What's a Royal Artisan?"

"The Royal Artisan lives in the palace and makes original designs of weapons and ritual items," Ba explained. "More importantly, the king funds all the work of the foundry."

"That's great news. We win, we survive. Hooray," declared Big Ming.

The Master Musician quietly asked. "Live in the palace? Is that a good idea for you, Jianjun?"

Ba darted a glance at him and shook his head.

What was that, thought Tangtun. *Is the king the killer? That makes no sense. Why would an old friend, even an angry one, be a killer?"*

Little Ming said to Tangtun. "They sound worried."

"They are, and with good reason."

"What reason?"

"Our fathers are worried that iron may put our foundry out of business. Then what would our village depend on?"

Little Ming said, "Oh-h-h. So that's it."

Tangtun said, "First, jobs might go away, and now, a killer might try to kill my Ba."

They sighed together. And then, Tangtun declared, "But, we're going to win and we're going to stop the killer, even if it's the king!"

"How will we do either one, especially if it's the king?"

"We'll figure it out. First, we need a really outstanding idea to win the contest." He chewed on his bottom lip. "And, we snoop more. Try to see or overhear something. Be sneakier."

“Sneaky? Me? I’m the king of sneaks!” Little Ming laughed at his own joke.

Tangtun grinned and stood up. “And, tonight we learn how to sword fight—for real!”

CHAPTER 6

Later that evening Tangtun and Little Ming trailed after Ba. Near the house, Ba turned around. "Are you boys ready to take up the sword?"

"Of course," shouted Little Ming. Tangtun nodded.

In the shed behind the house, Ba pulled swords from a high shelf and handed one to each boy.

"But your sword is long," said Tangtun.

"Short boys need short blades," said Ba, "at least until they are men. And for now your blade isn't sharp either, so you won't slice each other."

Little Ming danced around Tangtun in a circle swinging his sword in arm-length arcs, first over one shoulder and then the other. Then he jabbed at Tangtun. Without thinking Tangtun jerked his sword up and slapped the jab away. Little Ming lost his balance and plopped on the ground. They both laughed out loud.

"Enough!" said Ba. "Swords are serious instruments, not toys."

He pulled Little Ming up and said, "Now face each other and get ready to fight before you start swinging."

"Put your swords on the ground. Take a deep breath and swing your arms to relax. Fighting is intense, but the calmer you are, the faster you can be."

Tangtun felt as silly as Little Ming looked, shaking his arms and turning around. Struggling against gales of laughter, he almost choked.

"Now spread your legs so your feet aren't close together, and flex your knees. You need to be balanced, able to go in any direction. Like this." Ba assumed a swordsman stance and continued, "Hold your sword this way." Ba placed his thumb and first two fingers tight around the hilt and showed them his other three fingers were holding on loosely. Then he lifted his sword, close to the middle of his body with point up and leaning a little forward from his body. He raised his other arm slightly to balance himself.

The boys tried to copy the position, but Tangtun's sword wobbled. They both laughed out loud.

"Wait," said Ba. "I'm right-handed. You're not, Tangtun. Switch hands."

Tangtun switched, but his laughter still threw him off-balance and he fell to one side. Little Ming only laughed harder.

Ba dropped his sword-laden arm down beside him. "Stop!" he said sharply. "Give me your swords. We'll try this again another day." He turned and stomped into the house.

"That was fun," Little Ming chuckled.

Tangtun watched Ba leave and shook his head, "He doesn't think so."

Then he turned to look his friend in the eye. "Stop playing all the time. Maybe the killer is a swordsman and that's why Ba wants us to learn."

"Swordsmen are usually soldiers, or have been."

"Right, maybe even BaBa."

"Your Ba? Nuh-uh!"

"Ba has a really big sword and this morning a passing soldier knew him, so I wonder." Turning toward his house, he said, "Go home. Tomorrow we ask more questions. Somebody must know something."

CHAPTER 7

The next morning Tangtun dragged gray hemp pants up his slight frame and wriggled a tunic over his head and stepped around his curtain.

"Hey, Gege, Older Brother," sang out Meimei, a bowl of boiled rice in one hand and a drippy spoon in the other. Perched on the edge of their parent's low bed, his sister swung her short legs and drummed her heels. "Are you going to draw river pictures today? Or watch doves? Can I go with you, can I, can I?"

Tangtun shook his head and frowned. "I've got work to do, so don't bother my stuff again. Stay away from my paintings."

"Later can you play with me? You be BaBa. I'll be MaMa." She tilted her head with long black hair just like his and then crossed her button eyes. "But not with that face! You're stormy!" Tangtun raised his hands like bear paws and growled until she giggled, but he didn't join in.

Ma's lips lifted a little at their antics but hardly disturbed her somber face as she wrapped leaves around cold rice patties. Tangtun asked, "MaMa,does any worker at the foundry have a problem with Ba?"

She frowned at him and said, "Eat now. And, no more questions."

Tangtun raised his bowl near his mouth and shoveled in his breakfast with chopsticks. He heard his father clomping around outside, ready to go.

"I lost my baby tiger, Gege. Can you make another one for me?"

"Not now. I'm in a hurry."

Ignoring her trembling lip, he picked up his lunch and said to himself, I can't make toys today. I need to look for the killer."

Ma said, "Come, Meimei, outside with Ba's mother."

Turning to look up at Tangtun, she gave her usual instruction, "Learn something new today, my son." She didn't ask about the bruises on his arm or mention the nighttime conversation he'd interrupted.

At the door, he said, "MaMa, who might kill…?"

"Stop," she interrupted. "No such talk in front of Younger Sister."

He bowed his head to show he understood and took Meimei outside. She danced around him, saying, "Play with me, play with me." When she spotted their grandmother exercising in the grassless space between their house and the neighbour's, she ran straight at Nainai. Her arms were extended high and one leg lifted like a great blue heron. She needed only a little bump to fall hard.

"Meimei!" He dashed between them. "Be careful!"

Nainai smiled her thanks and then she stared into his face and asked, "What's wrong? Trouble with Ba again?"

"I can't please him, Nainai."

"There's more to your Ba than you know, Tangtun." She inhaled deeply and moved into a new position. Tangtun dropped his head in respect for her, wondering, does she know about the killer? No matter, she won't answer me anymore than MaMa did. Then he rounded the house, crossed the yard, and jumped the drainage ditch onto the narrow dirt lane leading out to the road.

Watching small brown birds flit limb to limb on the occasional bush, he clutched the charcoal in the small pouch tied at his waist. His fingers itched to draw the birds in flight. Thick clouds lying low across the wooded ridges behind the village seemed to push down on his chest. He dragged in a ragged breath and kicked a pine cone hard. It zipped down the road and lifted, carried along by the wind.

Beneath the crossbeam of the carved village gate, his parents caught up with him. MaMa laid her hand on Tangtun's shoulder, "Do you want to dye hemp with me today, my son?"

A thrill shot through his belly at the chance to get more dye for his paintings. He looked at his father's stiff back and said, "Gray turning sun yellow makes my heart sing." He almost touched his father's arm.

Ba moved away and spoke over his shoulder. "No need to think about colours, Tangtun. With me, you'll learn a man's trade."

A flush warmed Tangtun's face as he nodded goodbye to MaMa.

Taking two steps to each one of his father's, he caught up. "BaBa," he dared to speak again. "Who wants to kill you?"

"Don't ask so many questions, Tangtun. I told you before. It's adult business."

Tangtun picked up a rock, pulled his arm back with all his might, and slung it down the road. It's satisfying thud on a tree pushed him to speak. "I'm not a child. Next Fang Festival, I'll be thirteen," he said.

"So, you're old enough to be silent like you're told," BaBa said.

Tangtun threw another rock, kicked up a cloud of dust and thought, *I'm old enough to spy out who your enemy is, too. If only I knew more about him.*

CHAPTER 8

"Men do what men have to do."

All morning the apprentices moved ingots, ran to get more coal, cleared trash, and carried dross. The workers talked about how to win the Battle of the Artisans and the apprentices eavesdropped. Tangtun loitered near conversations, listening for any mention of anger or trouble, especially the killing kind.

"You know," said Red, banging away in the smith shop. "We made the first chariot axle blade and the king loved it."

"That's my kind of weapon," Little Ming said, whipping imaginary steeds. "Slash enemy horse legs, bring them down, and drive on untouched." He squatted and swiped his arm hard horizontally, and Tangtun jumped over his pretend blade.

In the woodworking shop, the carver stroked a reclining wooden deer with real antlers and spoke aloud to no one in particular. "What about a large statue of the state symbols, a wooden Chu phoenix with clawed foot holding down a Zeng wolf?"

"And make one ruler lose face?" asked the Master Musician on his daily walk through the foundry.

"We must win," Ba interrupted from where he stood watching the cauldron of copper and tin bubble. "Iron swords could ruin our business. With no foundry, our villagers have no work, and with no work, no village."

"Change like that takes a long time," Big Ming said.

"No one has the right furnaces yet to make iron swords for all the king's soldiers," said Red from near the smith shed. "They need time to build those. No need to worry yet."

"Maybe not," Ba said, "but we must win this contest to persuade the king to give us more work."

The newest foundry worker, stacking pattern blocks for the moldmaker, said, "What about something personal like a Royal Wedding Coin?"

"And the bride and groom can each wear half on a leather strap around their necks," chimed in Tangtun, "and find one another in the afterlife by matching halves."

"Never," said Ba. "King Wang is not a romantic like you, Tangtun."

Tangtun flinched and turned red, thinking, you're so mean. No wonder someone wants to kill you. And then he looked at the newest worker more closely. Why did he move to our village? Did he know Ba before he came? No. He's just friendly."

Little Ming drew everyone's attention by running in circles. "A girl has to catch me to put anything around my neck!"

Haohao responded, "Not Tangtun, he's always daydreaming or drawing. One day some girl's going to sneak up and catch him that way."

Everyone laughed.

Tangtun, still stinging from Ba's romantic remark, looked stern, "Be serious. We need a winning idea."

When the Master Musician walked over to stand beside Ba, everyone stopped talking. They always did when the Master spoke.

"We already make bells, bells that sing with two tones, across mountains and rivers, in earth and heaven, to the living and the dead. Let us fashion one great bell, the largest, most elegant ever made."

The metal script writer jumped in. "With the names of both kingdoms and rulers painted in gold."

"Add a powerful dragon for the groom and a life-giving phoenix for the bride," said another worker. Men and boys nodded.

Tangtun elbowed Little Ming. "I can paint great dragon heads with long bodies."

Little Ming poked him back. "Your BaBa won't let you. He hates your drawing."

The Master Musician patted the wooden pitch tuner hanging from his waist and said, "I will adjust the pieces, so even this Great Bell will be tuned to play two resounding tones."

Tangtun's father said quietly, "We agree then. We make a huge bell, but there's one last thing." He stood with arms folded and legs spread as everyone turned toward him.

"Because I'm the foundry leader, I'll take our entry to the palace for the contest at harvest time."

"But, Jianjun," said Master Musician stepping toward him. "You can't appear before King Wang!"

Without thinking, Tangtun sprang forward. "No, BaBa! I think he might kill you!" His cry yanked every worker's eyes toward him. "Let someone else go."

Ba dropped his arms and squeezed both hands into fists. From under scrunched brows, he bored Tangtun with a look. "You're right," he declared. "The king once swore he'd kill me if he ever saw me again, so I've hidden from him for years. But, I must do this—for our village." He swept his arm to include all the men, saying, "Everyone here but you," he held his open hand toward Tangtun, and continued, "Everyone but you understands that men do what men have to do."

Ba's piercing eyes and words propelled Tangtun backward as if he had been shoved hard. He turned on his heel and stomped off as hot as boiling metal.

CHAPTER 9

Near the cauldrons Tangtun filled buckets with dross the bronze maker had skimmed off the liquid metal. Bending down to get his shoulders under the bamboo rod, he balanced the two buckets. Pungent fumes from the furnaces burned his nose like the angry thoughts sizzling in his head. He brooded out loud to Little Ming every time he passed him.

"The king is the killer!"

"How can anyone win against the king?"

"BaBa will face him alone."

"BaBa always says '*du li nan zhi*, one person alone is not strong enough,' but he doesn't mean it."

"I could help. I could."

And, every time he muttered, Little Ming agreed, and Tangtun stiffened and glowered more.

Tangtun trod heavily and noisily toward the dump pile downriver from the foundry. On the far side of the pile, he saw Kai, one of the younger boys whittling a stick. The sun glinted off the polished knife handle. Tangtun dropped his buckets and the dross spilled in every direction. He dashed over to Kai. "You stole my knife!"

"I didn't!" he said hiding it behind his back. "I traded a good rabbit skin for this knife."

"Traded who?"

"Haohao."

"I should have known. Well, it's mine."

"Prove it's yours."

"BaBa put three mei on my knife like an arrow. I see them shining there. Give it to me."

"Get my skin back and I might give it you."

Tangtun ran with long hair flying through the foundry, jumping over pots ready for market, dodging around the cauldron, and kicking a stack of swords in every direction.

"Hey!" yelled the coppersmith.

Tangtun never looked back. He found Haohao sweeping up clay trimmings in the mold maker's shop. He slammed the bigger boy hard in the chest and shouted. "You stole my knife!"

"What knife?" Haohao stumbled back, his face as calm as a sleeping baby's.

"My special knife," Tangtun panted. "Where'd you get that rabbit skin on your belt?"

"Kai gave it to me."

"You traded my knife for that skin, thief!" He shoved Haohao again.

"I'm no thief," said Haohao, pushing back harder. "I found that knife."

"You found it stored in my treasure box," Tangtun yelled.

"Only girls have treasure boxes," Haohao smirked.

Tangtun threw his fist with all his strength and hit Haohao's nose. Blood spurted. Haohao jumped with both arms wide, grabbing Tangtun into a bear hug and squeezing so hard Tangtun's breath blew out in one big whoof. They both fell and rolled, screaming, kicking and pounding anywhere their fists could land. Dust flew everywhere.

Someone grabbed Tangtun's tunic and snatched him upright. The coppersmith pulled Haohao away.

"What are you two fighting about?" demanded Ba.

"He stole my knife!"

"Found it," shouted Haohao.

"Be quiet, both of you! Where's the knife?"

Kai stepped forward, holding out the knife, "I traded Haohao a rabbit skin for it."

Ba took it and said, "I made this for Tangtun. A man needs a strong knife to skin animals or defend himself," he said looking sideways at Tangtun, "even if he uses it in other ways."

Tangtun's eyes widened like a spooked deer. Great, now he's mad at me for carving things.

"Tangtun, here's your knife. Haohao, give Kai his skin back. All of you get back to work—now!"

Haohao sneered over his shoulder at Tangtun. "BaBa saved you this time. Just you wait, son of the boss."

Tangtun glared in return, stuck his knife in his waist pouch, and plodded back to the dross pile to shoulder his bamboo carrier again.

"Son of the boss?" he muttered with each step. "Favoured? Ha! BaBa knows I carve things with my hunting knife. He'll probably yell at me about that next."

But Jianjun didn't yell, because a neighbouring foundry soon challenged their contest entry.

CHAPTER 10

Several days later, Tangtun heard Haohao making a commotion near the ingot carts and headed that way. Haohao gestured as fast as he talked. "Another foundry is making a giant bell for the contest, too," he said.

"That can't be true, Haohao!" said Little Ming, stepping through the smoke billowing from a furnace.

"It is true," said Haohao. "My uncle cleans his morning catch with other fisherman down by the water's edge. He talked to a fisherman who has seen their bell."

The metal script writer spoke up. "It's no matter. The gold writing on ours makes it a grander memento of the wedding. We'll still win."

"They plan to paint their whole bell gold. It will shine like the sun," Haohao said.

That announcement silenced everyone except Ba. "Our foundry only gets gold with special orders of the king, but not enough for something extra like a bell," he said. "We may need something better to win."

"Right," Tangtun murmured to Little Ming, "what's better than a bell glowing with gold? We need an idea to keep my father alive and this foundry going."

"But how can we do that?"

"I don't know."

The next afternoon by the shed built across the back of the house, Tangtun showed his sister Meimei an old pattern block he had brought home for her.

She poked at three raised and evenly spaced round parts sticking up. "What are those?"

"*Mei*," he answered.

"They're named for me?" she asked.

Laughing, he said, "Uh-huh, your name means beautiful. This *mei* is different. It's like where the baby pigs drink milk from the mother pig."

"Here," he continued. "Help me press this soft clay all over the top of the block until it covers all three."

Meimei pushed with tiny fingertips and leaned on the clay with the heel of her hand.

"Now we take the clay off." Tangtun's newly recovered knife fit in his hand perfectly. He slid its point under the edge of the clay lifting the edges. Slowly he persuaded the entire slab to separate from the pattern block.

"Aw, it's pushed in!" said Meimei. "It's ugly!"

"That's how we decorate bowls at the foundry," replied Tangtun. "First, we make a clay bowl with 'pushed in places' on its inside. Next we set a solid clay bowl inside that bowl and pour liquid metal in between the two bowls. When the metal cools, we break away both bowls. What's left is a bronze bowl with *mei* sticking out of its sides."

Meimei frowned and shook her head. "Show me."

"I don't have hot metal, but I can make this clay slab turn purple all over except in three spots."

He reshaped the soft clay and pressed it into the bottom of one of MaMa's old pots. Next he pushed the wooden pattern block in until its corners sat tight against the pot. Its *mei* touched the clay, leaving space between the block and the clay.

Next he got some of the purple mulberry juice MaMa used to dye hemp and added some dirt and cold fat drippings from her cooking. He poured the thick, almost black mixture over the block and the clay, wiping his wet hand on the grass.

"The juice is covering everything except where the *mei* press against the clay," he explained. Then he covered the pot with a straw mat. "There. We'll check it in the morning."

After breakfast, Meimei and he raced behind the house to check their project. The juice and fat looked like mud. He tipped the pot sideways until the goo had oozed out on the ground. Then he lifted the pattern block straight up off the clay.

Meimei jumped up and down, exclaiming, "It's purple with dots! How pretty!" Grabbing the clay out of the pot, she ran. "I'm going to show Nainai."

When he got home from work that day, he saw Meimei playing out back. "You gouged out the dots on the clay," he complained. "Why'd you do that?"

"'Cause," she shrugged. "And, look! I'm filling my holes with the purple mush."

"Why?" Tangtun demanded.

"It's interesting," she said with a grin.

"You've messed up what I made you." He turned away with a disgusted sound, "*Sheesh.*" He took a few steps and then he whirled around, slapping his fist in his hand. "Wait! Meimei, you're so smart. Your idea might help us win the contest."

He dashed back around the house and slid to a stop just beyond the door, where Ba was swinging a bronze axe to break up wood for MaMa's clay oven. Words tumbled out of Tangtun's mouth.

"Let's not just write on the bells! Let's reverse the pattern block, carve each character into the wood." He twisted his fingers in a gouging motion. "When a character sticks out of the clay mold, it will make a character-shaped hole in the metal wall of the bell. And then we tap a little gold into the hole to make the writing sparkle as bright as the Great Bear in the night sky."

"Stop talking so fast, Tangtun," Ba said and leaned on his shovel. "You mean the writing is sunken into the bell?"

"Yes, yes!"

"No." Ba shook his head. Tangtun's heart thudded and his shoulders slumped.

"Putting gold into the characters would be much harder than simply writing on the bell."

"But, no other bell before has ever been marked in gold this way, has it?

"None has, Tangtun, but I'm not sure words cast into the bell can impress the king more than writing or painting them."

"But wouldn't the king like something new, and wouldn't a new idea win the contest?"

Ba raised his hand. Tangtun flinched, expecting a blow to stop his questions.

"He's having the contest to get something new," Ba said scratching his head, "but the script writer and mold maker won't like it. It makes more work for them."

Tangtun tried again. "Ba, it's a new idea. Can't you ask them if they will try it?"

Ba bowed his head slightly and said, "Yes, I'll ask tomorrow."

Tangtun went to his mat in his sleep corner, hugging himself and thinking, It's a good idea, Ba, even if you won't say so. Everyone will. I'm positive. And he drifted off to sleep.

CHAPTER 11

"A good father makes a clever son."

The next morning Tangtun, certain the workers would like his idea, paced back and forth outside the house, jumping over rocks, swinging a stick, knocking against tree saplings and swishing tall grass.

"BaBa," he called. "Can we go to work now?"

At the foundry Ba shared Tangtun's idea of casting characters into the bells and making them golden. The workers whose work would be affected most reacted.

The script writer hesitated. "That sounds like more work for me," he said.

"No complaints from me," the mold caster said. "Get me the pattern and I'll cast it."

The Master Musician stroked his beard. "Such an addition to the bell will affect the pitch of the two tones. I must tune each one again, but I can do that. Let's try it."

Ba gathered the rest of the men and told them Tangtun's idea. At first they reacted like Ba, but then Big Ming said, "It's new. We will win for sure."

Everyone approved and several said, "Good thinking, Tangtun."

Tangtun dipped his head without a word and felt satisfied like he had eaten a full meal.

"Back to work, everyone," Ba ordered.

Some workers shaped clay molds for the more than one hundred parts of the Great Bell. On special wooden blocks, the metal script writer began practicing how to carve out a character with no mistakes. Later, the character blocks would be used to make the molds for the parts of the bell with the writing on them. But the original hand carving was tedious and slow.

After several days, the worried script writer searched for Ba. Tangtun eavesdropped around the corner of the copper smith shop.

"Tangtun's idea of casting some of the characters into the bell wall is great, but it takes too much time. It's more complicated than carving out simple *mei,*" the script writer said. "And, you know, reversing what we usually do with the *mei* is so new, we don't even know its name."

Ba laughed and said, "You just described its name, *ming-ke.* See."

Tangtun watched him bend to scratch in the dirt with a stick.

"Carving characters into the pattern blocks is key to writing the names in the metal," he said, drawing a tall cross with a tent on top and two blades of grass on the ground at the bottom. Beside it, he drew a block with a slanted hat above it. Next, he drew a horizontal line cut with diagonal slashes and then a vertical spear and said, "First we cut with a knife, and then if we must, we carve late into the night." He looked up at the metal script writer and added, "Together these mean putting names into the metal takes time. We call the process *ming-ke* or inscribe."

"After casting characters in the bell wall itself, we add *jin,*" he continued drawing a table with a roof on a short pole for *gold.* "So, the carving plus the casting into the metal and lining with gold becomes *jinmingke*—gold inscription—the name of Tangtun's new process!"

"A good father makes a clever son," said the script writer.

Ba bowed his head toward the script writer and said, "You flatter us."

Feeling as if his body smiled all over, Tangtun jigged from one foot to the other on his way to the furnace to load his buckets again.

CHAPTER 12

One day while carrying dross to the foundry's edge for dumping, Tangtun saw Haohao squatting by the river, dipping and pouring water. "What are you doing?" he asked. Haohao continued to dip and pour water over his arms. Then he stopped and scratched and rubbed his face and his arms.

Walking over to look closer, Tangtun stopped short. "You have really big red spots! What happened?"

Haohao looked up with tear-filled eyes, "Your mother says it's the lac tree sap. Just walking by the bowls being lacquered poisoned me, I guess." He scratched some more. "I'm waiting for your mother to bring her shellfish medicine."

"You're funny-looking," said Tangtun.

"It's not funny," said MaMa from behind him. "Run along now, son, while I put medicine on Haohao to cool his skin."

Nearing the furnaces, Tangtun said, "Hey, Little Ming. Did you see Haohao? He's got big watery blotches all over and scratching like a wildcat."

"I saw him. He must have done something bad." Little Ming laughed.

"MaMa says the lac tree sap has caused his damp heat."

"Then he better stay away when they start dipping the wooden pieces for the bell stand." Little Ming chuckled, too.

"At least we won't be bothered by him for a while."

"He may be meaner than ever."

Big Ming said from the furnace, “Stop laughing. Be glad your mother can help him.”

“Where are his parents anyway?” asked Little Ming.

“And, why does he talk to me the way he does?” added Tangtun, even as he remembered how Haohao sounded almost like Meimei on the riverbank.

Putting an arm around each of their shoulders, Big Ming pulled their heads near his and said, “Haohao lives with his uncle because his parents couldn’t afford to keep him. They had nine children already, so they sent him away.”

“Oh,” Little Ming and Tangtun said together, their laughter gone.

“He’s negative all the time because he wishes he had parents like you two. Remember that.” He pushed them away. “Now go back to work.”

Tangtun walked on, trying to imagine MaMa and BaBa giving him away, but his shoulders twitched, and his mind darted away from the idea. And, why would Haohao want a father like his anyway?

He passed Ba talking with the metal script writer again.

“We have a more serious problem than slow, hard, casting of script in the bronze. We can’t let any other foundry discover our new idea. We must guard our work to keep it secret until the contest.”

“Agreed, Jianjun,” said the metal script writer. “Don’t worry about our men. They won’t talk.”

"Ha! Everybody talks," grunted Ba, "and good news travels fast. From now until the contest, I better sleep in the foundry to keep any outsiders from seeing our bell."

Sidling up near them, Tangtun cleared his throat, swallowed hard and risked asking, "May I stay in the foundry with you, BaBa?"

"That would be more work again. I'll have to watch out for thieves and you, too," Ba said at first, frowning.

"But, Ba..."

Ba sighed and said, "Since inscribing the bell was your idea, you can stay." He started to walk on and then stopped. "But, first, you need to know how to handle yourself in a fight. Go get Little Ming and your swords."

"Right, Ba. We'll practice every night from now on."

Tangtun ran to tell his friend about protecting their secret and taking lessons. In a few minutes, with chests heaving, the boys skidded to a stop in front of Ba. He lifted his sword and said, "Ready?"

"Ready!" they chorused, swinging their swords upright.

CHAPTER 13

A few days later, Little Ming and Tangtun took a wooded path home after work. They zigzagged back and forth across it, each whopping a stick on everything they could reach—big rocks, little rocks, bushes and tree trunks. Tangtun banged hard and chanted, "Got to win, got to win."

Little Ming changed the chant to, "Yes, we do, yes, we do." Tangtun chimed in.

"So," said Little Ming, stopping still in the middle of the path, "are you sure we are going to win?"

Looking at the ground, Tangtun slid his foot back and forth, piling up the dust. "I don't know," he said. Then he lifted his head and stared at Little Ming. "We have to win and keep BaBa alive at the same time—if he'll let me help."

Ping! Thud! Ping, ping, thump! Tangtun drummed and chanted. "We've got to win," Little Ming echoed, "Win, win."

"Ar-tists win, win con-tests."

"Sons fight, fight for fa-thers."

They thumped and chorused, "Win, win, fight, fight!"

Their path led up to the road to the village. There they hit old willow baskets and pieces of clay pots resting under bushes. Squash, swi-i-ish, tappity, tap, tap! "To-gether wins bat-tles. Togeth-er we'll win—Bat-tle of the Art-i-sans!" Bam, bam! Boom, boom, boom!

Tangtun grinned, listening to the pitches change. "The pot shards sound like the chime stones at festival time, don't they?"

Little Ming smiled back and lifted his elbows with his hands swinging free. "Hanging on that long limb, they sound like ring-necked pheasants talking in the fields—clack-clack, clack-clack."

Tangtun laughed out loud at his gyrating arms. "Yes, and other times they roll like thunder! Ka-bo-o-o-m!"

Little Ming spread his arms, dropped his voice, and shimmied. "Thunder I feel deep in my bo-o-o-nes."

"But it's best when Master Musician adds all nine bells," Tangtun said. He smiled at the memory of hitting the bronze bells himself sometimes when no one was around. Their hanging with gaping, arched mouths seemed a silent invitation to make them speak.

"He strikes stones and bells fast as lightning."

"Right," said Tangtun. "He hammers bells with one hand and chime stones with the other. They sound like all the birds of earth singing to heaven at once. Like this!" He tapped his stick faster and faster on three different sized rocks and a broken bronze horse bit on the side of the road. Clack! Ping, ping! Ping, ping, ping! Clack! Clack!

"*Ai-yah!*" Suddenly Tangtun jumped around like a bee had stung him. He shouted, "That's it, Little Ming! One giant bell won't win the Battle of Artisans, but a whole set of bells will, like a company of soldiers win a battle! Let's tell BaBa."

They ran the rest of the way home, burst through the door, and slid to a halt in front of Ba. He sat astride a low stool, re-braiding a rope for tying bundles.

"Where've you been?" Ba asked.

Too excited to answer, Tangtun's words and hands flew like a whirlwind. "I have an idea. Listen! Fifty bells, a hundred bells—let's make a gigantic number for the contest."

"More than anyone has ever made before," added Little Ming, gulping air beside him.

"One hundred bells? Impossible." Ba never looked up.

"But we'll win, we're sure of it!"

"Uh-huh," Tangtun's father grunted and kept braiding.

Tangtun's raised eyebrows said, "*Huh?*" to Little Ming who shrugged, "I don't know." Tangtun shifted from one foot to another.

At last Ba dropped his hands and spoke. "Your idea as usual means more materials and more work." He sighed, shook his head and again began braiding new hemp into the old.

"Another outrageous idea."

Tangtun's sunny feeling disappeared as if a cold wind had blown through the house. He made a silent vow to himself, I have good ideas. One day I will find one you approve of, BaBa.

CHAPTER 14

Bang! Bang! Bang! Rumble, rumble. Grind, swish. Gurgle, splash! The sounds of work rose above the foundry. The bronze makers melted ingots of copper and tin together into molten bronze following Jianjun's formula for their contest entry, the largest bell they had ever made. For two days, Tangtun kept hard at work. His head hurt from having one idea to win the contest after another and rejecting it without telling anyone, not even Little Ming.

Everything stopped when the Master Musician walked up from the riverbank where Jianjun and he had been in deep conversation. The workers gathered round him.

The Master spoke. "You know, a bell set might win the contest."

Tangtun sat down hard on the ground unable to believe his ears. Little Ming plopped beside him. "He's talking about your idea."

"Shhh," Tangtun said. "Listen."

"Do we have time to make a set?" asked one worker.

"How about the biggest set ever made?" said the village elder. "It could win the contest."

One worker said, "We know you imagine new things, Master, like kite spies flying over enemy armies."

Another said, "And, you can make many bells sing."

"The biggest set is a new idea," said a third.

"A good idea," said Big Ming.

"Maybe. How many bells can we make?" asked Red, the coppersmith.

Haohao landed beside Tangtun on the ground and grunted from under his shaggy hair, "Your dad should know. Why isn't he talking?"

Tangtun couldn't speak through the amazement that had frozen his tongue. *Ba told the Master Musician about my idea!*

The Master said, "Since nine is the most we've ever made, let's plan for sixteen bells—a set of three, a second set of six, and a third of seven bells."

Everyone began firing how-to-do-it questions.

"How much time would we need?"

"Can you tune that many bells, Master?"

"Do we still need the big bell?"

Ba spoke up. "Our Great Bell can be entered as a promise of our gift, the largest bell set for the royal wedding."

The mold maker said, "One bell alone has one-hundred pieces. Sixteen require many more sizes and molds. I'll start working on those right away. Then when our one Great Bell wins the contest, we'll be ready to make more."

"I must change our mixing formulas, so the bells can play the new tones the Master must add," mused Ba.

"Making many different bells will take more time," said the caster, "but, we should be able to finish them all in less than a year."

"Yes, we can, but first we must finish our contest entry—the biggest bell, the most impressive of the set, one that can win," said Ba.

"I agree."

"Let's do it."

Determination walked with each man and boy as he headed off to do his part for the Great Bell. All the while everyone puzzled over how to make the largest set of bells in the world.

They still yelled for Tangtun to fetch and carry and sweep and clean up.

"Tangtun, hurry."

"Apprentice, over here."

"They don't know a big bell set was your idea," Little Ming said to Tangtun.

"*Uh-uh,* no, they don't, but BaBa knows." Satisfaction rang in his voice.

That evening, Ba said, "Boys, get your swords." Tangtun and Little Ming ran.

When they came back, Ba raised his sword. The boys slid apart, one to his right and the other to his left, and held their swords upright in the middle of their bodies.

"Point your sword toward my eyes," he instructed. "Tangtun, when I thrust at you, step back with your right foot and bring your hands down to your waist at your right hip. Little Ming, you're right-handed so you do the opposite. Keep your sword up so you can make mine miss you. Don't reach out. Just make me miss you."

He thrust his sword at Tangtun. Tangtun stepped back but tangled his feet and went down. Little Ming howled with laughter. Without stopping, Ba turned and thrust toward Little Ming who immediately jabbed back, completely missed Ba's sword, and stumbled past him.

"You're both dead," said Ba dropping his sword arm.

"So, every night without fail, we practice until you take this seriously." And, he walked away.

Tangtun stomped his foot. "That's it, Little Ming. Don't come for lessons any more. In fact, stay away from me. I have to learn to fight, so I can help save Ba!"

He swung around and marched into the house, leaving Little Ming standing in stunned silence.

CHAPTER 15

Night after night Tangtun tried to use his sword the way Ba taught, but he couldn't seem to master it. Exhausted, Ba and he ate their supper and then curled up on their mats in the foundry. They lay close together for warmth in front of the partially complete bell covered with a large cloth made by MaMa.

Each night Tangtun watched the stars moving across the sky and scratched in the dirt what he saw—a flying fish, a crane, and many more. He knew that the Great Bear never disappeared but turned in a circle. His tail had almost moved below the moon's path. Soon it would be harvest season and time for the contest.

One night a thud and muffled curse startled Tangtun awake. In the darkness he felt his father's hand holding him still. They moved not a muscle.

Swu-ush, swush. The sound of several feet sliding on dirt came from their left. Three silhouettes grew large against the star-lit sky. In one swift move, his father stood straight up, faced them with legs spread apart, and demanded in a loud voice, "Who are you? What do you want?" Tangtun stood up beside him, his sword and knife in hand.

"We came to see what's so special over here," one man sneered.

"Hear you've got a winner for sure," added another man towering over the first.

Ba eyed the silent squatty third, inching around to sneak past them to get to the bell's hiding place. "You won't see our entry until the contest," he said. "Get out, while you can."

Tangtun tensed his body and bent his knees. The five stared at each other. Who'll move first, wondered Tangtun.

The three yelled at once and rushed Tangtun and Ba with raised weapons. One had a long bronze rod, another, a knife, and the third a sword. Tangtun stumbled and fell when his father shoved him back out of the way and raised his own long, double-edged sword. With a short, fierce jab, Ba hit the arm of the short man coming from his right side. His knife flew across the room. Quick as a striking snake, Tangtun stuck out his foot, tripped the defenseless man and sent him sprawling on the floor where his head hit hard.

With his heart pounding in his throat, Tangtun sprang up and kicked away the thief's weapon. He stood over the downed man, ready to stick him in the throat if he moved. His eyes darted from the thief to BaBa.

Ba's braid flew around his head as he spun away from a blow, jumped on a bench and blocked a swing from the tall, skinny swordsman. He sliced at the advancing rod wielder, who dropped the rod, clutched his arm, and backed away with blood pouring through his fingers. Dodging a thrust from the sword wielder, Ba stepped down and deftly engaged him in a tense duel.

To Tangtun, it seemed his father never stopped moving, turning and stepping. With each stab and swipe of the sword, he moved in a determined dance with his opponent. Swinging harder, Ba advanced. Desperate now, his opponent tried to defend himself, fighting a battle he had already lost.

When the downed man sat up shaking his head, Tangtun raised his sword, gestured with his knife, and ordered, "Move over by your friend." Like big angry cats, the two men crouched, ready to spring at him.

"Don't even think about it," he barked, surprised by the fierceness in his own voice.

Just then BaBa jabbed the swordsman in the armpit, disabling his arm. He dropped his sword and backed away.

"Get out of here!" shouted Tangtun, waving his weapons at the thieves. All three turned and raced out of the foundry.

Ba sank on to the bench, breathing hard, his forehead on his hands that gripped the sword hilt. Tangtun sat down beside him.

"You're a Master Swordsman, BaBa," said Tangtun with glowing eyes.

"I'm ordinary," Ba said. He put a hand on Tangtun's knee and said, "You helped, but why did you let those men go?"

Tangtun shrugged and changed the subject. "How did you learn to fight like that?"

"A long time ago, in another lifetime." BaBa sighed. "I thought I left it all behind me."

Tangtun asked, "Were you a soldier?"

Ba sat up and leaned his sword against the bench. "Yes, going to war for my king was the most glorious thing I could do," he said.

Tangtun hefted his father's long bronze sword in his hands and asked, "Why did you stop?"

"It's a tough story, Tangtun," Ba said, sighing and swiping his brow, "Do you remember we talked about the Battle of Ying one day?" He bit his lip and said, "I fought in that battle and my life changed forever."

For the next half hour, Tangtun listened to the hair-raising tale of the battle of Ying, part of a war fought by his father and his father's friend, the prince, long before Tangtun was born.

CHAPTER 16

"Kill that traitor!"

Later Tangtun slept on his mat. His breathing quickened and his eyes darted under his eyelids. Grappling to take in Ba's story, Tangtun's mind dropped Little Ming and him into the middle of his father's battle. Best friends fought side by side.

Sword held high, I spur my leather-clad horse at a warrior atop a huge gray.

He swings his halberd at the prince's head.

I slice his arm off with one blow.

Another soldier hacks at me. Little Ming knocks him from his horse.

My heart beats hard.

"Du li nan zhi," I shout.

"One alone is not strong enough," the prince yells.

Arrows fly. Swords clank. Spears thud. Men scream.

Dirty, bloody sweat clogs my nose.

I can't breathe.

Black and red leather armoured bodies crumple.

More and more fall.

"Retreat," I yell.

The prince repeats, "Retreat, retreat!"

We ride hard away from the river.

At the city wall, Little Ming and I head at the soldiers again, swinging our swords.

Horses squeal, bodies fall.

"Inside, close the gate!"

Enemies rush after us.

I tie a brush bundle to an elephant's tail and light it. I tie and light more.

Trumpeting, crazed elephants run straight at the enemy.

"Soldiers are coming over the city walls!"

"Stop them!"

"My father," Little Ming shouts.

We run.

"Save me," says the king. "Save me."

The king's face changes to my grandfather's face.

"Save me," grandfather says.

I run home.

The king screams, "Kill that traitor!"

Feet pound behind me. I lurch around corners. Run faster!

"Stop, Tangtun!"

I pump my legs. They hurt. Footsteps close in.

"Tangtun, Tangtun!"

Someone grabs my leather vest. I'm caught.

I jerk. I thrash my head.

I yell. My throat is paralyzed. "Hel-el-elp-p-p-p...."

"Tangtun, Tangtun!"

With his heart pounding and breath gasping, Tangtun jerked his arm away from the hand on his arm and dragged his eyes open. He saw his father leaning over to shake him out of his nightmare. "Bad dream, Tangtun?"

"I was fighting your battle, BaBa, and almost got caught." Sitting up, Tangtun rubbed his eyes and asked, "The king you betrayed is dead, so why does our king want to kill you?"

Returning to his own mat, Ba said, "After we lost the city, the king retreated and the ruler of Zeng hid him. Later that Zeng friend helped him regain our capital city. I fought in that battle, too, so, instead of killing me as a traitor, the king banished me. But, he forbade my ever returning to the city."

"It's good then that his son, your old friend, is king now?"

"Wang thinks I'm a coward and a traitor for saving my parents instead of his. Even though the father showed me mercy, the son swore to kill me the next time he saw me."

"And, no one can change his mind?"

Ba shook his head. "He's not the friend of my youth. He has become a power-hungry ruler in the years since I disappeared from Ying."

"Hmm," Tangtun said, thinking, even if we fight sometimes, Little Ming would never kill me.

"Is that why you work in the foundry?"

"Your mother convinced me her village foundry had honourable work and was safe. So, I moved my parents and her here and studied bronze work with her father before he died."

"I'm glad," Tangtun spoke with a soft tone. They both sat in silence until he asked, "Isn't our life better than fighting wars all the time?"

Tangtun saw the tightness in his father's face as his head shook side to side. "Tangtun, peace is best, but not one of those thieves tonight came in peace. They were ready to fight and fight they did." With his jaw set, he hit Tangtun's knee with his fist, emphasizing each word. "Because I know how to fight back, I beat them. I protected the secret of our bell."

Tangtun drew within himself, trying to avoid the fierceness, and said, "It's good you used your sword, I guess."

"You must fight, too. A man can't let other people do his fighting for him."

Remembering his dream, Tangtun took a deep breath, turned cross-legged on his mat and looked straight at his father. "But, sometimes letting someone else fight for you might be needed."

"A man always fights for himself."

"You risked your life for your parents during the Battle of Ying. Now, you risk it again for our foundry. What happens if King Wang attacks you at the contest?"

"When we were children, I almost always defeated him; I can again."

Tangtun breathed deeply and blurted out his idea. "Let me lead the men to the contest, so he won't see you."

"Never," Ba jumped up. "King Wang may find out you're my son and kill you! You don't know him."

With the strength of his dream soldier self, Tangtun stood up. Ba stood toe to toe with him. Tangtun stared up into his face without blinking. "Like you, I, Elder Brother, can help protect my family."

Ba locked eyes with Tangtun for a full minute. Neither one looked away. Then Ba nodded. "*Du li nan zhi.*" One man alone is not strong enough. You are Elder Brother. But, Master Musician already volunteered to lead the team to Ying with me. You see, I plan to disguise myself as a mute."

"Disguise? The king will know it's you."

"My beard will be long by then, your Ma knows how to make my hair gray, and Master will speak for me. As long as Wang doesn't hear my voice or get too close, he won't know it's me."

He lay back on his mat to end the discussion. With a huff of anger, Tangtun did the same. He vowed to himself. I am going. I will think of a way.

CHAPTER 17

The foundry buzzed with excitement. Their entry for the Battle of the Artisans was ready. The mold makers and casters had finished every part of the bell, molding and casting again and again until they fit one hundred pieces together into one big bell. The Master Musician used all five strings of his pitch tuner to be sure the bell would ring two golden tones. The goldsmiths had beaten their one small gold nugget and tapped it into the cast characters until they flashed in the early morning sunlight.

Four muscular men strained and grunted, lifting the bell, heavy as a young water buffalo. They laid it on its back in the middle of a farm waggon and braced it with thick tree limbs. Feeling dwarfed by its size, Ba and Tangtun climbed in. With Little Ming's help, they tossed MaMa's soft golden hemp sheet ballooning up and over the bell. Then Tangtun and Little Ming dropped down together and stepped away from the waggon. Ba mounted his horse and the Master Musician joined the driver upfront.

The driver flicked his whip to start the horses on their half-day journey to the palace, in the heart of the capital city of Ying. All the workers brushed the Great Bell with their fingertips for luck as it moved past them. The apprentices ran alongside.

Haohao heckled Tangtun. "Good thing you're not going, Tangtun! You would probably fall down bowing to the king!"

Tangtun's insides chilled at the picture, but without a tremble, he yelled over the rumble of the waggon and horses, "Never happen, Haohao!" He grabbed Little Ming's arm. "Come with me!"

"But I thought you said stay away from you."

"Never mind. We do everything together. Come on!"

They dropped back from the other boys and dashed through the foundry to a short-cut footpath winding up the bluff to the village. With legs and arms pumping hard, they ran as fast as they could, jumping over rocks and once even a slithering snake, and straightening out curves when the undergrowth cleared enough. As the path grew steeper, they pulled themselves up by holding on to saplings.

At the village gate, Tangtun snatched up the bedroll he had hidden earlier, said, "I have everything we need in here," and kept running on the road to Ying. They ran past the turnoff to the Master Musician's house and on uphill. Near the top of the bluff, the road angled sharply upward and narrowed into Elbow Pass, just wide enough for one waggon. Breathing hard, they pushed their way inside a thicket of scrub oak bushes beside the road and collapsed.

"Perfect place, Tangtun," Little Ming said.

Then, as their panting slowed, they heard the waggon coming.

Ba rode ahead of the horses to encourage them, two workmen on foot walked to either side of the horses holding on to their halters and speaking softly, "Come on, Horse," and, "Pull,

Horse, Pull." The driver whistled, clicked his tongue and yelled, "Giddy up!" The burdened horses strained in obedience on the steep incline. Everyone was watching the road ahead.

"Ready?" asked Tangtun.

"Ready!" answered his friend.

The waggon passed by and the boys scrambled through the bushes to the road and ran for the waggon. Grabbing the back gate, they pulled themselves up and over into the waggon without a sound. Tangtun lifted the bell cover and Little Ming scooted underneath it and into the bell itself. Tangtun slid right behind him up against the bell and spread the cover out again.

"Made it," whispered Little Ming.

"Yes, now be quiet until we get to the city."

"Then what?"

"Not sure. I'll think of something."

They settled in for the ride, but Tangtun couldn't resist lifting the cover and looking about. Soon they passed rice fields dotted with water buffalo and hat-shaded workers, tending the late crop of plants with golden heads. Hong Lake to their right soon disappeared in the low haze hanging over it. Smaller lakes, ponds and streams shone like mirrors and the sun shone bright over the Jianghan Plain. Green mountain sentinels lined its distant edge. Once in a while, a yellow or orange and brown tree broke all the green, announcing that the cold season would arrive soon.

Tangtun looked out one side of the waggon and then the other. Just as he said to Little Ming, "I want to paint pictures of this beautiful land," a waggon-wheel dropped into a hole. Everything lurched to the right, including the bell. "Oh-oh!" cried Tangtun, sliding with it.

"Whee!" Little Ming's voice echoed inside the bell.

Tangtun tried to grab the bell, but he snatched the cover instead as the waggon driver cracked his whip and shouted at the horses, "Pull!" The waggon jerked forward and Tangtun rolled into a tangle of limbs and fabric. Little Ming spilled out of the bell with his legs spread-eagled.

The driver shouted at the horses to pull, once, twice, and the waggon swayed first left and then right. Tangtun whipped his arms around and kicked his feet this way and that to get free from the cloth. When he stood up, his feet shot out from under him and he rolled against the bell. A brace snapped with a pop like a tree limb in an ice storm and the bell slid into Tangtun, trapping him against the back gate of the waggon. He tried to scoot out, but the bell held him tight. The waggon shifted again, the bell leaned away from him a bit, and he took a deep breath. A sharp pain shot through his right side and he cried out, "Ow!"

CHAPTER 18

Little Ming stood up and shrieked, "Tangtun's hurt!"

Ba heard that yell and reined his horse in a tight turn and rode close to the waggon. Then he jumped from his horse and landed beside Tangtun. With legs spread and every muscle straining, he held on to the sliding bell to keep it from striking him again.

Then a booming order from the driver propelled the grunting horses forward. Their lunge bounced the waggon level again. It landed upright in a cloud of dust and Ba, Tangtun, and Little Ming all settled in the bottom with a swooshing breath of relief. Ba leaned over Tangtun and moved the hand clutching his side. When he pressed the spot, Tangtun cried out.

"Relax, Tangtun," he said. "You've cracked a rib. We need to strap it with something."

The Master Musician bent back from the seat, holding out his long outer robe. "Use this."

While the other men found a tree limb to replace the original bell brace, Ba tore long strips and wound them tight around Tangtun's upper body several times. Sweat popped out on Tangtun's brow. "You'll be fine by the time the moon comes out of its heavenly palace and goes to sleep again," his father said, "but you can't swing a sword now."

"The rib won't interfere with my sword-arm," Tangtun grunted.

Ba climbed out of the waggon and mounted his horse. Looking down at the boys, he said, "I told you not to come with us."

Tangtun and Little Ming looked at one another ready to argue against being sent home.

"But we're too far along to send you back home. I'll think of what to do with you for the contest."

As he clicked his tongue at his horse to go, he said over his shoulder, "Actually, it's good you kept the bell on the waggon."

Tangtun smiled a little and settled down on the floor with Little Ming, hoping he would be able to breathe deeply soon without hurting. More and more carts and riders loaded with tradable goods joined them on the road to the largest city on the Plain. Ba rode and talked.

"Tangtun, you boys stay outside, nearby but out of sight, while the Master Musician and I take the bell into the palace."

Tangtun frowned but didn't dare disagree, so he shrugged the shoulder on his good side. "Yes, BaBa," he said. "I'll do what you say."

His father continued, "You're not dressed for the contest and your hair is not braided."

"But MaMa made us special robes, too," said Tangtun. Seeing the surprise on his father's face, he rushed his words. "'Cause she felt sorry for us not because she knew our plan."

Ba shook his head and sighed. "Well, then, both of you braid that long hair and you can go inside with us. But, remember," he said in his tree-bark tone, "remember, King Wang demands respect. When he arrives, drop to your knees and put your face on the ground. Don't get up until the royal guard knocks his spear handle against the ground."

Tangtun pressed both hands against the sharp jabs in his side caused by the waggon jolts. He tried to laugh when Little Ming asked, "Do we have to put our faces in the dirt?"

"Everyone kowtows. You stay down until the Master stands up," said Ba. "And, be quiet. When our team presents our bell, only the Master speaks. You don't make a sound. No one ever interrupts the king."

Tangtun said, "Sounds easy. We'll remember."

"I'm not so sure, the way you ask questions all the time."

Tangtun asked, "So, what if we accidentally do something wrong?"

"Pay attention, Tangtun! And, whatever happens, do not tell him you are my son!"

Tangtun said, "I won't." But even in the sunshine, determination couldn't overcome his cold dread that Ba's disguise wouldn't work either. What then?

Ba reined his horse closer to the waggon and leaned down to grip Tangtun's arm. "I'm not happy about any of this, but we have to do it. The King Wang I knew long ago would never hurt you, but now, well, just be careful. Do everything the way I've told you."

Tangtun's insides shook and his ribs ached and he was tired of hearing instructions. So, he nodded at his father looming over him and said, "You can trust us."

CHAPTER 19

With his sword strapped to his saddle, Ba rode with lips drawn in a straight line. Tangtun kept a hand over his broken rib to ease the hurting. A slight breeze and their familiar silence mile after mile began to soothe his nerves.

Tangtun's eyes roamed from one sight to another. They passed hemp fields and vegetable farms. Huts and workshops with smoke curling upward dotted the rolling hills. Then he spotted the wall of Ying crossing in front of them from left to right.

"Little Ming, look! The city seems bigger than anybody said."

Yellow-leaved flame-of-the-forest trees shining with pink seed pods stood beside two massive wooden doors that loomed over them.

"This is the main gate your father told us about," Little Ming said when they drove through.

"Yes, and a thousand people must live here. No wonder three of the ten gates are to let water in."

Tangtun stared down street after street lined with earthen houses topped with thatched roofs. Splats, thuds, and scrapes of earth being rammed into wooden frames filled his ears. On one corner stood a house almost finished and next came a side street lined with new houses in different stages. Tangtun's head turned from side to side, taking in details to share with Nainai, MaMa and Meimei later.

"This place is so big, BaBa!"

"It is and growing, too."

People chattered and pans clattered in every direction. Tailors sewed leather pants. Shopkeepers displayed tunics and pants, farm tools, cooking pots, and even hunting knives, bows and arrows. Vendors sold fresh food from carts—here leafy greens, there a pile of rice to measure into women's baskets right next to stacks of raw meat red with blood. A warm fish smell joined earthy odours to make Tangtun's nose twitch and his stomach growl.

"Driver, stop. It's time to eat." Ba dismounted next to a rotund man in an apron who circled a pan of fresh fish over fiery coals. He bought food for the team.

Tangtun and Little Ming tossed the hot morsels from hand to hand and then chewed with their mouths open, drawing in cool air. Licking their fingers, they stared at a nearby stone-craftsman's shop displaying shiny pieces of polished jade, amethyst, and agate. Tangtun itched to rub their smooth surfaces and hold them up to the sunlight, so their rich colours shone through. But Ba was ready to move again.

"What are those, BaBa?" He stared at a vendor with strange wares spread on a blanket.

"Horns of rhinoceroses and elephant tusks," Ba clenched his fist and flexed his arm. "They grind the horns for medicine to make men strong."

"*Ai-yah*," Tangtun said, almost gagging at the idea of swallowing ground-up horn potions. "Anyone who eats that must already have a strong stomach."

Little Ming laughed and turned to Ba. "Maybe Tangtun needs some now in case he has to defend himself."

"He won't have to fight, Little Ming," Ba said.

Tangtun, holding his side, said, "I can fight if I have to."

"Not with that broken rib, you can't. If something happens, I'll do your fighting for you," Ba declared with his hand on his sword hanging from the saddle.

Remembering how his father had fought the thieves in the night, Tangtun sat taller and ignored his pain. He nudged his bedroll lying at his back to be sure his sword was still there,

Their waggon followed horse-drawn carts. Men in cropped leather pants and women with billowing hemp wrap-around skirts bustled about their business, filling the streets. Boys chased each other, weaving through the crowd. Some people stopped to stare and point at them, but most ignored them.

Master Musician said, "See that red silk banner with the golden, leaping dragon sewn on it?"

The boys saw it flying high above another gate in an interior wall.

"It flies when King Wang is in the palace compound," said the Master.

When their waggon joined the line of craft persons arriving for the contest, Ba told the driver, "Pull over here." He dismounted and tied his horse to the rear of the waggon and got out his roll. He pulled a sack out and then sat, leaning against the wheel out of sight from passers-by.

The boys peered over the side of the waggon as Ba began to dust his long beard with white clay powder. Next he bent over and put an entire handful of the powder on top of his head and spread it through his hair and over his braid. A white cloud rose around his head and without warning the boys both sneezed together and fell back into the waggon laughing as hard as they could.

"Boys," said Ba.

They looked toward the side of the waggon and their mouths fell open. An old man they wouldn't know stared at them.

"You must forget I'm your father," he said. "You boys stay close and keep silent. Remember everything I told you about how to act with the king."

"He really does look like an elder uncle," said Little Ming.

Tangtun only nodded, unable to force words through his tight lips. *Maybe, just maybe, Ba's disguise will work*, he thought. Pulling his shoulders back, his chest out, and his chin up, he ignored his throbbing side. He stared straight ahead as the Master Musician said, "Let's go. We have a battle to win."

CHAPTER 20

Inside the palace wall, artisans from all over Chu region moved steadily past the royal gardens glowing with golden chrysanthemums and tiger lilies. Their waggons and carts carried covered contest entries—balls, rectangles, domes, dwarf-size and giant-size lumps.

"What have you there?" they repeatedly called out to each other.

"The winner, of course!" Tangtun and Little Ming answered, and everyone laughed jittery laughs.

Tangtun and his team circled a lake with long, leafy branches of weeping willows making lazy waves above a family of rhinoceroses playing in the water's edge. They passed elephants walled off in a corner of the grounds and a caged tiger pacing back and forth. Tangtun scrunched up his nose at the acrid odour of droppings at the same time his fingers curved reflexively into his drawing position as he pictured himself drawing the animals in this peaceful setting, dotted with colour and motion.

Approaching the red-tiled wooden palace decorated with yellow, blue and green animals and birds, he grinned. "What a colourful building! I've never seen wall scenes like those before," he said to the Master Musician. Knowing artists lived in the city gave it a homey feeling for him, too.

When the waggon drew up to the palace, the team lifted down the bell without disturbing the cover and carried it up many steps into a great open courtyard. Tangtun followed with the long stick for playing it.

Contestants arranged their entries in the most favourable way before a red-columned platform holding the Great Seat of the King and a gigantic gong. People crowded the courtyard, laughing and talking, basking in the afternoon sun, happy to join the contest. Young servant girls in long blue wrap-around skirts and tunics moved among the crowd carrying trays of tea.

Master Musician spoke. "Take our bell and its stand near the front on the left, hang it on the stand without removing the cover," he said. "Then change into the team robes."

"Right away," said the men, following his orders as if he were Ba, who stood without speaking beside the Master.

Tangtun pulled two sunrise orange robes out of his bedroll and handed one to Little Ming. They switched them for their tunics. Tangtun tucked his sword in the waistband of his pants, where he could easily grab it if necessary. Braiding his hair seemed to twist his insides tighter and tighter.

They all followed the Master Musician and Ba inside. The boys took their place just behind their team. Remembering Ba's instructions, Tangtun promised himself he'd stay silent. His knees shook and his hands sweated as he waited for the king. He accepted tea from a servant, gulped it, and watched for the king to appear.

Finally a royal servant strode in front of the crowd, struck the gong and announced, "Bow before the Son of Heaven, King Chu Hui Wang!"

Everyone dropped to their knees and put their foreheads on the ground. Pain ricocheted through Tangtun's ribs hard when he bowed. He stopped part way, holding himself up with the stick and pressing his hand against his side, unable to breathe.

"I can't..." He looked up just as his father snapped his head around and glared at him.

"Quiet," the Master said pushing Tangtun farther down.

Tangtun gripped his sword hard and bit his lip to keep from crying out in agony. He concentrated on the sound of leather-shod feet marching together to both sides of the platform and stopping at exactly the same time. Thud, thud, thud went a spear handle on the ground. When the Master and Ba stood, Tangtun and Little Ming joined them. The pounding in Tangtun's side slowed to a dull ache. Everyone stood in complete silence.

Above them in an oversized armchair draped with a cloud of golden cloth, the king sat in a wine-coloured robe with knot fasteners and embroidered cuffs and hem. Several stern-faced advisors flanked him. Three fierce-looking military guards stood statue-like in black and red leather armour on each side of the platform. They held halberds, long spears with—not one, but three—dagger-axes added.

"They look fierce," said Little Ming out of the side of his mouth.

Tangtun answered the same way. "King Wang looks scarier than any of them."

"Yes, a smile might crack his leathery face."

Ba glared at them with a look so familiar, Tangtun worried, how can the king not know that face?

Everyone turned left to watch a short man stride into the room. He carried a flat musical instrument twice his height that he sat on a low stool. With clasped hands, he bowed low before the king, faced the crowd and bowed again, then to the right and to the left.

"It's Master Zigong," Tangtun murmured to Little Ming.

"Quiet," Master Musician said.

Zigong spoke in ringing tones. "By poetry one arouses the mind, by ceremony, one regulates character, and by music one becomes accomplished."

Then he sat with his instrument across his lap and began to strum its seven strings. Soon the strumming changed to a melody that sent a strange shiver along Tangtun's spine.

Time will pass us by.
The sun sets each day but it will rise the next morning,
The flowers fade each year, but they will bloom again the next.
The beautiful birds fly away and are nowhere to be found.
My youth years fly away just like the birds.
That is how it is, that is how it is.
My youth years are nowhere to be found.

The crowd stood in complete silence when he finished. Even the king stood up while Zigong walked slowly to his seat beside the king's ministers.

"What was that?" asked Tangtun.

"The qin is the favoured instrument of our sage, Kongzi," answered Master Musician. "Zigong sang a song of Kongzi's home village to remind us that death comes to us all."

Chills ran down Tangtun's back. He stood straight and tall and whispered to himself, "No one dies today, not if I can help it."

CHAPTER 21

Everyone watched as a servant entered and marched to the centre of the room and declared, "Let the Royal Battle of Artisans begin!" Bowing toward the king on the platform, he continued, "Son of Heaven, I present first the craft persons of Long Wan."

Two men dressed in black robes with box-like hats walked forward from the back of the crowd with arms raised above their heads. Soft silk panels hung down from the rod they held. They stopped in front of the king.

"Lord," they said, "We bear handmade wall-hangings symbolizing the union of the great kingdoms of Chu and Zeng. Such hangings can honour the Son of Chu and his bride, the Royal Sister of Zeng, at the wedding celebration and then in the home of her father."

The banner bearers turned in a slow circle and the servant continued. "The painting on the left portrays the Son of Chu, the dragon of royal power. The one on the right shows the Daughter of Zeng, the immortal phoenix who renews life. May their union, and ours, last forever!" Then the bearers bowed, took their gift to the left of the Great Seat and walked with steady pace back to their place. The crowd murmured their approval.

Tangtun breathed out of the side of his mouth again. "Our bell is much better than wall-hangings."

"Shush," said the Master.

"Next," said the servant. "The Artisans of Songzi have prepared an entrance guard for the wedding hall and later the palace of the King of Zeng. This mighty guard will keep the prince and princess safe from any demon spirits who try to bring them harm."

Four purple-robed men carried horizontally between them shiny black wooden panels stacked on top of each other. With a flourish they stood them upright before the king. The men took one step sideways, unfolding the pieces so they became four. They towered over the heads of the men.

"Ooh," said the people, smiling at one another. An ornate carving of fantastical animals and flowers in deep red lacquer stretched across the left pair of panels facing its twin on the right panels. Then the men stepped in perfect unison in a circle so everyone saw the exquisite pictures repeated on both sides of the screen. "Ah-h-h," exclaimed the crowd.

Tangtun risked another whisper. "Can you tell if the king approves?"

Ba flipped his hand fast in his direction, and the Master Musician said, "Quiet!"

While the men folded the screen, set it next to the first gift, and returned to their places, the king's servant announced, "Our next festival gift is from Jiangling, the home of embroidery."

Tangtun looked left and then right, trying to see the Jiangling craft persons. The crowd parted for two short women in sophisticated gowns who seemed to float forward, carrying a shiny box atop a rosewood stand. They set it down before the king and one opened the box with an elegant wave of her hand. The other lifted out a golden yellow silk ball, the most beautiful Tangtun had ever seen. Delicate needlework in the colours of the rainbow formed an intricate pattern of paired birds and flowers around the ball. Its long red silk tail hung down between her elbows as she held it up before the king.

"Oh, Great King, the embroiderers of Jiangling shared hours of happiness preparing for you a Royal Unity Ball, symbol of love and family. We offer you this wedding tradition of our village, a symbol of friendship between the Chu and the Zeng peoples."

She turned with the ball held high above her head with its soft tail flowing across her wrists, down one forearm and off her elbow, like a waterfall. Again the crowd said, "Ooo." The women bowed low, lifted the ball and stand and carried it to its place in the line of wedding gifts.

The servant announced, "Now, the Artisans of Houma!"

Tangtun stiffened. "This is the team we must beat," he whispered to Little Ming underneath the rolling sound of the Houma team's entry.

With muscles bigger than Ba's, four bare-chested men in leather aprons rolled a covered stand in position in front of the king. They caught the four corners of a matching leather cover and lifted it off with a snap. A large golden bell with a collar of greenery topped with fresh red peonies—the flowers of riches and prosperity—stood before the king. In the bright sunlight, the bell shone like the sun itself! King Wang didn't even blink.

"What a beauty," said Little Ming

Everyone shielded their eyes from the light reflecting off the bell. Whispers went all around. "We're looking at the winner for sure."

"Is it solid gold?" some asked.

"It's only painted with gold!" said others.

Tangtun spoke to the worker next to him. "It's more splendid than Haohao's uncle said. Maybe our bell isn't that impressive."

"But ours is more unique."

"Be quiet, both of you," hissed the Master. "You insult the king."

Tangtun clinched his teeth and thought that they must have something more to win, but what? He wrinkled his brow as he puzzled over what he could add.

The Houma worker addressed the king. "Son of Heaven, we have made a shining golden beauty to represent the union of our two great regions."

The King questioned, "Can such a fancy bell even make a sound?"

"It can," their leader replied. He swung his long wooden stick, striking the centre of the bell and a deep tone resonated throughout the palace, down one walkway and then another. Before it died away, he hit the bell with several quick little strikes on the side and shorter tones floated over the crowd. In the total silence that followed, the men turned the glowing bell in a slow circle, set in the gift line, and moved back to their place.

Only then did the crowd break their awed silence, talking and gesturing to one another in obvious excitement.

Tangtun dropped his head and shoulders and groaned. “How can we ever beat that?”

The whole team, even Ba, looked sadder than he had ever seen them, as if they, too, had given up completely.

CHAPTER 22

"Who is your father?"

Just then the royal servant looked at the Master Musician and announced, "The Artisans of Jingnan!"

Tangtun said to the team, "We will win this!"

He gestured at two team members who leaned down, caught the bottom edge of the embroidered hemp cover facing the king and rolled it slowly up and over the top of the wooden bell stand. The king saw their bronze-ware entry before anyone else. Protruding *mei* decorated the bell in a repeating pattern. When light struck its middle panel, the king leaned forward squinting against the sparkling characters pricking his eyes with golden light.

Master Musician, as if he were home in their village, commanded the attention of everyone in the room. "This Great Bell exists for a most momentous occasion, the wedding of our prince." Pointing at the characters, he said, "It is inscribed with the names of our Majestic Ruler, King Wang, and the Marquis of Zeng, two men who show us how to live together in peace."

Whispers began to go around the room. "Inscribed?" "What is inscribed?"

"It is also inscribed with the names of the bride and groom and the year of their marriage. On the top—also cast in bronze—are a phoenix and a dragon, symbols of peaceful unity."

"What is this 'inscribed' you speak of?" queried the King. "Never have I heard such a term."

Master asked, "May the worker who created this inscribing show you, O King?"

The King did the unthinkable. He stood and walked forward to examine a contest entry up close. People backed away.

If he gets too close he'll recognize Ba, thought Tangtun, taking in a quick breath. But then the Master gestured for Tangtun to explain inscribing. Tangtun looked at his father, who barely nodded, but his eyes screamed at him to be careful.

With heart pounding, Tangtun bowed toward the king and traced a character with his finger, explaining, "We carve and mold the characters first and then cast them into the metal. We line each with gold. We write in the metal, instead of on it."

Someone nearby said softly, "But the painted gold bell is the best."

"Something new is better," said another bystander.

"It's the first of a kind."

Tangtun heard with pride the people speaking and added, "We reversed the patterns that traditionally make decorations stick out, so they would sink into the metal. We've done something no one else ever has."

The Master silenced Tangtun with a look and finished, "So, now we have the occasion of this gift written in the metal."

The king looked unimpressed, like Ba when Tangtun explained his latest idea. He said, "Let me hear if it sounds as auspicious as your description."

Tangtun held his breath, handed the bell stick to Ba, and watched the king for any sign of recognition as his father stepped in front of their Great Bell. Gripping his heavy stick like a boatman's pole, he struck the centre lip of the bell. Without moving, it reverberated with a single low-pitched rumble. Then he swung his stick to hit the side lip of the bell, following the first pitch with another even lower. Again, Ba rocked his whole body to swing his stick against the centre lip, raising its low growl into a thunderous boom. Then he struck the side lip faster and faster, pleasing every ear.

The Master spoke over the dying tones. "O King, this bell is great, but it is not alone. It is king of a family of bells, more than ever before."

"A fami...?"

With a strong voice, Tangtun interrupted the king. "Thirty-two bells, the most ever."

Everyone breathed in quickly, at a mere boy misbehaving so. The team's jaws dropped open at his doubling the sixteen they had planned. Ba took a step toward him with a stony face and drawn eyebrows.

"You have spoken once too often," the Master Musician warned, gripping Tangtun's arm.

The King ignored his impertinence and looked from one to the other, shaking his head. "The wedding is half a year away. No one can make that many bells in six moons time."

Without releasing Tangtun's arm, the Master spoke. "We compete today for a team, a team prepared to deliver the complete bell set for the royal wedding."

The idea of teamwork made Tangtun speak up again. "We can do it because *du li nan zhi*. One alone is not strong enough."

The king stopped moving and stood still and stiff as a stone. His face reddened and he shouted at Tangtun. "What did you say?"

"Now you've done it," said the Master.

With the skin on his back trembling like a horse bothered by flies, Tangtun repeated, "One alone is not strong enough."

The king stared at him for a minute without moving a muscle and then said, "I've heard that before, a long time ago."

Tangtun heard his father suck in a sharp breath, but he didn't dare look at him. Watching King Wang swipe his hand across his face, shake his head, and mutter, Tangtun slid his hand under his robe to grip his sword, ready if the king made the connection.

The king seemed to argue with himself, "Never mind."

He started toward his seat. Then he stopped, turned back and glared at the Jingnan team. Tangtun stopped breathing. "Sky Father revealed to you how to write in metal, so you can put the names of Chu music notes in the metal, right?"

Tangtun bowed and straightened with the Master who said, "It is possible."

"I wonder," said the king, dismissing them with a wave of his hand.

Wound tight as a snake about to strike, Tangtun couldn't think as they moved their bell in line with the other gifts.

CHAPTER 23

More teams presented impressive entries. One woman modeled a sixteen-segment jade pendant of dragon-phoenix design while another team displayed a red-lacquered suitcase with all twenty-eight constellations on it. A square bronze bowl had four fantastic dragons crawling around it with their heads sticking above a wine jar in the centre. The team said blocks of mountain lake ice around the jar would keep wine fresh. The crowd continued to ooh and nod with each new item added to the row of gifts.

Tangtun fidgeted and shifted from one foot to the other beside his Great Bell, telling himself, every entry is terrific, but our bell has to impress the king the most.

Then determination stilled him. *It must, it will win for our foundry to survive.*

At last, King Wang gestured to his advisors to follow him. As he inspected each wedding gift, its creators all bowed and tried to overhear what his advisors were whispering to him. When he stopped beside the Jingnan bell, they too bowed to the ground. Tangtun strained to hear what the king and advisors were saying but caught only a word or two. Their faces revealed nothing when they ran their fingers along the inscriptions.

Finally the king returned to the Great Seat, turned around and raised his arm. He declared in a loud voice, "I accept your gifts as praiseworthy examples of Chu creativity and tradition. They honour the deep friendship between my father and the father of

Marquis Yi, and they shall all represent Chu people well in a royal wedding display."

He stopped. Everyone froze, wondering, *But who's the winning team and the new Royal Artisan of the Chu*?

He dropped his arm and said, "Marquis Yi of Zeng is both an artist and a musician..."

Tangtun's eyes widened with that news and his chin went up.

"…so I need a gift worthy of his status and interests."

Tangtun stiffened from head to toe but was unable to unclench his hands or slow his racing mind. *Choose us. Say we won. Make Ba the Royal Artisan.*

The king continued. "The Marquis has a large collection of musical instruments, and he loves novelty and variety. I must give him something no one else can." He lifted his arm toward the shining bell, paused and said, "The winner is," and he paused again. "The winner is the team from the village of Jingnan."

Tangtun's whole body shook and his knees almost gave way when the nearest workman slapped him hard on the back. Everyone stood and cheered and crowded round to congratulate the team.

Then King Wang stood once again. Into the ensuing silence, he bellowed with a scowl, "Now. Young man, what was that you said to me earlier—one alone is not strong enough?"

Tangtun looked at the Master for permission to speak. "Yes, Revered One."

"I knew another boy a long time ago who always said that. His name was Jianjun."

Tangtun froze in place, his hands fisted tight.

"Who is your father?"

Tangtun's heart leaped in his throat, but he answered with a level voice. "Sir, your friend, Jianjun, is my father."

"You're the son of that scoundrel? He is not my friend. He deserted my father at the Battle of Ying," the king shouted. "Where is he now?"

Without even glancing at his father, Tangtun lied, "At home in our village," and thought, *I have to keep him from looking at BaBa.*

He grabbed at his sword, trying to free it from his robe, and turned with his eyes darting, looking for the best way out. Six soldiers jumped forward with axe halberds lifted, ready to pin him to the floor. The crowd all drew in their breath and backed up as one. Sweat popped out on Tangtun's head and slid down in front of his ears and the back of his neck.

Scowling, the king ordered, "Young man, put your little sword away. You're impulsive just like your father always was."

He stomped back to his chair and dropped into it, talking to himself. He stared into the distance as if he were alone. Tangtun and the guards lowered their weapons. Everyone else froze and held their breath. Then the king lifted his arm, with his open hand aimed toward Tangtun, and spoke.

"You tell Jianjun, your traitorous father, your team must do all that you have said—and more. I demand not thirty-two bells, but sixty-four."

"We can't make sixty-four..." Tangtun gulped, stumbling backwards. One worker shook his head while another dropped to his knees and groaned. Even Master Musician drew in a sharp breath. Ba showed no reaction, but Tangtun knew that meant he was steaming mad.

Waving his arms, the king continued. "The marquis is a nobleman. He must have instruments lining three walls in tribute of his status. And, I want all the bells in..., in...what is that word?"

" 'Inscribed'," an advisor said.

"Right, I want those bells inscribed with not only Chu music but that of the Zeng also." He marched back and forth. "And, your musicians cannot play just any wedding song. They must play an original one for the springtime union of Chu and Zeng."

Tangtun gasped and his stomach slammed his spine like he had been slugged. He looked at Little Ming, and the Master, and Ba and they all looked as stunned as he felt. He thought—*More writing, a new song, musicians—we don't have any musicians. How can we ever do everything he demands?*

The king paused again. Then he added in a stern, slow growl, "The royal wedding happens at the same time as Fang Festival, in exactly six moons. When the Great Bear's tail points toward the home of the morning sun and the four celestial horses of Fang appear to the right of the planting sun, our royal wedding time arrives."

Turning his pointing finger straight at Tangtun, he said. "Understand this. You cannot humiliate the Great King of Chu.

This bell stays here until you return with the full set for the wedding. Or, Fang receives you and your father as a sacrifice!"

Tangtun's mind reeled while the weight of doom pushed him into a bow with the crowd until the king left the courtyard. Even the throbbing of his broken rib failed to cut his choking fear. *What have I done?*

CHAPTER 24

As the team left the palace, Tangtun hung back until they were ahead of him. Then he dashed around the corner of the building and ran all out toward the far corner of the palace grounds. Pushing through the bushes and swinging around trees, he ignored his aching rib and slid down next to a shaded fence to catch his breath.

A guttural grunt made him jerk up. On the other side of the fence, two rhinoceroses rolled in a sunny pond. At his gasp, they looked his way, rose with mud dripping from multiple folds of thick skin, and then lumbered farther into the water and swam away from him. Their horns pointing at the sky seemed disdainful, like the rejection Tangtun expected from his father and the whole village.

"I should have bought some of that rhino horn medicine in the market," Tangtun said to himself. "Then I might be a stronger person."

He leaned his forehead against the fence rail until he dozed.

***

Meanwhile, outside the palace wall, the team stood staring at the ground, like no one knew what to say. The Master Musician spoke first. "We won. That's a good thing."

Everyone lifted the corners of their lips a little but said nothing. Ba said, "Yes, it is, but how can we ever do what the king demanded?"

As if a dam had broken, words poured out of everyone.

“…he said four times as many bells…”

“…and who knows how many characters in gold…”

“…even an original song…”

“…we’ll never finish on time…”

“…might all lose our jobs?”

“…your son has made our work impossible…”

“...he told the king who he is!”

“...and even drew his sword!”

“…both of you might die!”

Ba looked from one to the other. Turning to the Master Musician, he said, “Where is Tangtun? Did the guards take him?”

“No ...”

“He left with us.”

They all turned around, looking in every direction. Master Musician said, “He must have gone out another way.”

“There is no other way out,” said Ba.

“I’ll go look for him,” said Little Ming. “He probably just wanted to be alone.”

“You mean he couldn’t face me,” said Ba, sighing. “Go look for him, Little Ming. No one should pay any attention to a small boy, but be careful.”

Little Ming slid past the grumbling men and joined some stragglers of the crowd admiring flowers in the palace courtyard. He looked around, puzzled, where would Tangtun go? With his eyes on the guards, he scooted from tree to tree, moving toward a building behind the palace. Safely there he could see the garden shrubs and trees beyond and ran there.

"Tangtun," he called in a low voice, "Tangtun!"

"Here," Tangtun answered.

He followed the sound to the pond and stood beside Tangtun, who said, "I'm really in trouble with BaBa now, huh?"

Little Ming nodded. "Your father told us not to speak to the king."

"We wouldn't have won if I hadn't."

Little Ming stared at him, shaking his head.

Tangtun went on as if he had to tell the story even though Little Ming had seen it all. "When he asked me who I am, I had to tell him. He roared so loudly, I was sure he'd kill me, so I got ready to fight."

Little Ming's mouth and eyes rounded into big circles. "You scared me to death."

Tangtun continued. "He told me to put it away, just like a little kid." He rubbed his face with both hands. "Why do I always say the wrong thing at the wrong time?"

"You really did it this time," said his friend. "And now the king demands much more for the wedding gift."

"I know. We'll never be able to do it all. I can't face my dad after what I've done. As soon as it's dark, I'm going to find the army and be a kite spy for sure."

Little Ming studied the rhinos for a while. Then he spoke. "You know, Tangtun, I admired you when you decided to return home to help your father. But, now, I'm not so sure."

"I'm still your friend, the same person I've always been," said Tangtun.

"My friend is an upright son," said Little Ming. "He'd face his father."

The memory of the story about fathers and sons seemed like a stab in Tangtun's chest. He almost growled. "And, say what? Instead of protecting you, Father, I told the king right where to find you!"

"Yes, but the king also told you how to protect your father—make the bells."

Tangtun sighed and shook his head. "It's an impossible task and if we fail, we both die."

"Your ideas helped us create the winner in the first place," said Little Ming. "Now, you can help us all make those bells in time for the wedding. I'm sure of it."

When he saw Tangtun's turned-down mouth straighten into a fierce line, he knew his friend had decided, so he said, "But first, how can we get out of here without getting caught?"

"We'll swim out," said Tangtun, climbing over the fence. "That pond water must come in through one of the city water gates. Follow me!"

CHAPTER 25

Tangtun and Little Ming dripped their way along the wall toward the main gate. They could see Ba stomping in a circle, rubbing his bowed head, kicking up a dusting of clay powder. The team spotted them and yelled.

"Tangtun," said Ba turning toward him with a face of stone. When Ba raised his hand, Tangtun ducked slightly, but then he realized his father was only quieting the men.

With a nerve twitching near his eye, Ba gripped Tangtun's arm and spoke low, "I trusted you. You're old enough to follow orders."

Though he didn't say it, Tangtun heard, and act like a man, like me. He pulled his arm loose, stood tall and said. "BaBa, you're right. Soon I'll be thirteen years old."

Ba stared at him.

"I know I told the king where you are, Ba. And, I've made more work for everybody." Seeing the tight-lipped men muttering, swapping glares and turning away, Tangtun rushed on, "But I'll help us meet the king's demands."

Ba said, "You say that now." He shoved Tangtun toward the waggon.

"Right," said the workers, "more big talk from a little boy."

Ba pushed Tangtun's shoulder again, and he fell against the side of the waggon. "What happens when you get tired or when you want to draw something instead of working? What?"

Without answering, Tangtun pulled himself up into the waggon, dropping down next to Little Ming who landed just ahead of him. He pressed his flat hand over his throbbing side and whispered, "*Ai-yah!* Nothing changes."

"It will," said Little Ming. "It will."

"What's done is done," said the Master Musician, silencing everyone and climbing into his place next to the driver.

Ba mounted his horse and had the last word, "What the king demanded we must do—no matter what happens."

Riding home, Tangtun twitched and twisted on the hard waggon bed. Huts and fields, other travelers, the mountains and lakes that so fascinated him on his first ride to the city of Ying—all now passed like silent ghosts. The muggy air pressed down on him, making his skin feel as clammy and uncomfortable as his insides. Night fell and stars began to appear one by one.

He looked up at the dark sky when Master spoke. "Great Bear's three-starred tail already points where the sun sleeps."

Tangtun remembered his grandmother's star lessons. "Nainai said Old Bear is telling farmers it's time for harvest."

"True, Tangtun." Ba said from his horse. "Because of you, a hard job has become harder. When old bear next turns toward the morning sun, we must have four times as many bells ready for a planting time wedding, or else."

Wincing from the slap of the words as much as his side throbbing with each waggon bump, Tangtun said, "Can't we work faster?"

Ba slapped the reins on the horse's back. "Impossible. Maybe we can postpone some ordinary jobs or make fewer everyday pots. When cooler days come, work gets faster…" he paused.

Tangtun shifted in his seat. His bottom couldn't find a place to settle down any more than his aching side or scurrying mind.

"…until bear turns and dumps icy rain or snow on us. It's really hard to work in the cold."

"Hot furnace fires always warm us," Little Ming said.

Ba nodded. "We'll do what we must until Great Bear turns again. You and I will either live or die."

"We won't die, BaBa." Tangtun's firm sound and tight jaw made it a promise.

Ba did not answer. Twilight fell, the discomfort in Tangtun's side dulled, and he relaxed into the swing of the waggon and the clip-clop of the horses' hooves. Too ashamed to think anymore and tired of trying so hard with BaBa, he settled into the rhythm of the ride.

CHAPTER 26

The next morning Tangtun decided to put his long, unruly hair in a braid like the other men. Ba, his braid and beard back to their normal black, made no comment. Instead, he calmed the sour-faced foundry workers with a plan for making the bell set.

"We suspend all jobs except emergency ones. We build extra furnaces and anything else we need. You all know how to do your work. I expect each of you to do what you do best."

And, everyone did. Throughout the remaining days of fall, they worked until the sun went down and stars began to twinkle. Tangtun's rib healed so quickly he forgot it had ever hurt. And soon after every evening meal, Little Ming and he practiced sword fighting.

The foundry became an even dustier, smellier beehive of noises, movement, and voices calling out to each other here and there. The carpenters made dozens of wooden pattern blocks for groups of bells in sizes drawn out by the Master Musician. Carvers cut out characters naming each bell's position in the set and its two sounds. Using the pattern blocks, mold makers made and baked clay molds for casting. Ba oversaw the mixing of metals according to his new formula. Finished bell parts were reheated and hammered together, scraped and shaved, smoothed and polished. If a bell made the wrong sound, it was melted down and recast.

One day Ba said, “No one has ever seen a musical instrument the size of our bell set. It’ll weigh as much as six water buffalo. To hang such a set, we must build a suitable rack.”

So, carpenters designed two frames, whose hundreds of pieces fit together like a puzzle, and two beams, two almost twelve feet long, two over twice that, and two small ones. Hammers banged, chisels slid and thudded, and wood dust swirled.

Molders and casters added hangers shaped like the curled end of a grapevine to the bells. But to hang the heavy bells on the bottom of three levels, they created large crouching tigers with clawed feet. They cast posts of bronze warriors with swords on their hips and arms raised to hold the larger wooden cross beams and solid columns to hold the upper rack.

The Master Musician wrote out thousands of characters about Chu and Zeng music. The metal script writer huddled with him every day planning where to cast characters into the bells and fittings and which characters to carve into the rack of layered lacquer and line with gold. Others they would simply write with gold. Later, workers would repeatedly dip the rack pieces in lacquer until the waterproofing covered every character, a terrible-smelling process that burned noses.

The sun came up, they worked and worked, the sun went down. The moon awoke, came out of its heavenly palace, moved across the sky twenty-eight nights, and slept again, twice. The racing of the days drove everyone to a frantic pace toward a deadline that seemed ever more impossible to meet. With rain and snowy days coming soon, everyone felt success slipping away. Almost no one believed they could finish the bell set on time.

Tangtun moved slower and slower, filled with dread every day. One afternoon he noticed a strange silence hanging over the foundry. "BaBa," he said, "Something's wrong."

Ba strode to the middle of the foundry and saw men everywhere clustered in twos and threes, talking in low voices. Turning to Tangtun, he said, "Strike the lunch gong" and Tangtun rushed to obey. At its beckoning, workers came from all parts of the foundry and gathered around Ba and Tangtun.

"What is the problem?" asked Ba.

Red spoke for them all. "The Master Musician and scriptwriter say we won't have enough gold for all the inscriptions King Wang ordered. He will kill you both."

Tangtun's knees felt weak every time he heard the word kill, and then he got mad.

"He won't," said Tangtun and Ba at the same time. Tangtun stared as his father continued. "I own a small amount of gold."

Everyone looked at each other, murmuring.

"I give it for our bell set. It must be enough."

The workers whooped and banged tools on clay, wood, and metal items nearest them, sending a wave of relieved approval through the air.

As Red squeezed Ba's shoulder, Tangtun shook himself out of his shock. "Gold, BaBa? You have gold? How? Where?"

"Quiet. It's family business."

Spinning away, he said, "You talk too much. Talking makes more trouble."

Stunned, Tangtun stared at his departing back.

CHAPTER 27

"How can I make it up to them?"

Plodding into the yard at home behind Ba, Tangtun stretched his arms high, trying to relieve his sore muscles. He had lost count of how many loads of ore he helped put into the furnace today. And, everyone had seemed quiet and hopeless, all trying to think of ways to speed up their bell-making process and worrying about the gold. Stepping in the door, he knew he had to know more about the gold.

MaMa sat at a table in the corner, shaping rice dough into fat rolls. Her usual greeting, "Did you learn something new today?" made Tangtun wince. If you only knew, MaMa, what a hard lesson it was. He pictured her dancing later to silent music, swinging and twisting the rolls into long, skinny noodles and folding them into the pot. The possibility of disappointing her made him ache.

When he didn't answer, she said, "Didn't you say you have some jade lily tree leaves to soak? I'll heat some water for you."

"Not now," said Ba. "We're doing something more important."

"I learned we have gold, MaMa."

Ba sighed.

"I know we have gold. When your Ba left the army, he sold his uniform, his horse, everything but his sword, for gold. It's not much, but gold it is. We hope for a chance to buy back his father's land."

"Grandfather had land, where?"

Ba continued the story. "My parents' mountain home lay next to the king's summer palace. King Wang and I spent all our growing-up summers together, and the king treated us both as sons. When we were old enough, we joined the army. Then the Battle of Ying happened. When King Wang's father banished me, he also seized our family land."

Tangtun could hardly believe his ears. "Do we have enough gold to buy it back?"

"I hope it's enough to keep us alive."

MaMa's hands stilled and her mouth dropped open. "What?"

Ba ignored her, led Tangtun to the edge of the bed and bent over. At the bottom corner, he slid his fingers along until he reached a crevice in the bed and pulled. A piece of the bed fell away revealing a leather pouch in its hollow centre. He drew the pouch open and shook two gold nuggets, each one quarter the size of a small walnut, into his palm.

Tangtun looked up at his parents with glowing eyes.

"Is it enough, BaBa?"

"Yes, after we melt it."

"Enough for what?" asked MaMa.

"For all the writing about music that King Wang demanded," said Ba.

"But we'll have nothing, no gold, no land, no hope," she said, dropping both arms with her mouth turned down and starting to cry.

Tangtun stared from BaBa's gold to MaMa's tears and couldn't decide which he felt the most guilty about. *This is my fault*, he thought. *How will I ever make it up to them?*

CHAPTER 28

The next afternoon the dying sun tipped the tree tops with gold, while the darkening woods around the house seemed forbidding. *I can't get any more tired than this,* thought Tangtun, as he plodded across the yard to the shed built across the back of the house. He shivered in the dying light and inspected the shiny, dark green leaves he had spread on a shelf to dry. One time he had found a lacy leaf on the riverbank that had nothing left except its see-through membrane and tiny branching stem structure. So, he decided to try boiling away the green of the leaves to speed up what nature did slowly. If it worked, he would draw on the filmy leaf with MaMa's dye, to make a surprise for BaBa, a surprise about BaBa.

Hopefully my art pleases him, Tangtun mused to himself.

Checking the leaves for breaks or holes, he chose the most perfect ones and returned to the house. Dropping them into the steaming water, he sat the pot aside and draped a willow rug over the top of it. Before sleeping, he would heat the cooled water again and let the leaves soak overnight and tomorrow morning repeat the process before he went to work.

"Now find your sister, and get Nainai. We'll eat soon," said Lin.

He strolled around outside looking for his sister. Under a tree the chicken pen sat high up off the ground to keep snakes out. Every morning when MaMa let the chickens out, they scratched away every blade of grass and plant, making a perfect clear spot all around the pen. Mei loved to play house there, lulled by their friendly clucking, but no Mei was in sight now.

Haohao was bagging the putrid droppings to take home to add to his uncle's vegetable garden.

"Hey, Haohao, did you see my sister?"

"I wasn't looking. Girls bug me." He never stopped working. Tangtun ignored him.

"Meimei," Tangtun said. "Where are you? It's time to eat!"

Only the wind in the trees answered him. The waving grass between his house and Haohao's house drew him toward the path that cut through to the neighbouring field. Mei often hid from him there, shielded by grass taller than her two feet height.

"Come on," he yelled louder. "I don't want to play 'Find the Phoenix' with you! I'm hungry!"

He wound along the twists and turns of the path until he came out into the neighbour's field. Gathering clouds made darkness early and threatened snow. Having trouble seeing along the edges of the woods, he hugged himself against the cold. No sign of his sister there either.

Maybe she's with Nainai.

He reversed his route and raced back toward home.

His dwarf-sized grandmother, with white hair knotted in a bun on top of her head and with her jacket-clad, crooked back bending her over the stick she used to steady herself, crossed the yard in front of him. She stopped short when he asked, "Nainai, is Meimei with you?"

“I haven’t seen her since your MaMa came home,” Nainai said.

“Where is she?” Tangtun wrinkled his brow and listed places in his head, while he held Nainai’s elbow and they stepped into the house together.

“I can’t find Meimei anywhere,” he said, pacing back and forth.

“I told her to play near the house,” said Lin, wiping her hands on a cloth.

“Let’s go look again,” said Ba, getting up from his stool near the cooking fire.

“But BaBa, she wasn’t with Nainai or in her playhouse or on the path to the field. And you told her not to bother me in the woods anymore, so she’s probably not there. I’ve searched all her usual places. Something’s wrong!”

Tangtun breathed short and fast, willing BaBa to take charge.

Ba put down his pipe. “You’re right, Tangtun. Go up the lane to ask the neighbours to help us. I’ll go down the other way. We’ll meet up back in our yard.”

CHAPTER 29

Tangtun ran like the wind from one neighbour's house to the next, banging on each door and shouting. "Meimei's lost! Come help us. Bring lights." Their square, weathered, dirt-gray houses looked tired and uninviting, but he knew that each held caring people.

Old Mr. and Mrs. Chan grabbed their jackets, while Grandma Li shooed her son and his wife out their door with, "I'll watch the children. Go!"

Mrs. Yu was closing her tea shop, ready to go home. She turned in the opposite direction when she heard him. Haohao's uncle tied his water buffalo to a post in the field. A fisherman dropped the nets he was mending and joined the carpenter, heading down the road toward Tangtun's house. At the last house, Tangtun spun around and rushed home.

People milled around outside, talking in low voices. "How long has she been gone?" one wanted to know.

"When did you see her last?" another asked Lin.

Someone else whispered, "Those clouds look thick. Soon heavy snow starts."

"Maybe she curled up somewhere and went to sleep," said Little Ming.

"My yelling would wake her, silly," Tangtun said. "And besides it's too cold."

"She's hiding somewhere, just playing a game. That's what girls do," Haohao sneered.

Tangtun glared at him in disgust. "A lot you know, Haohao," he said.

"It is good you are all here," Ba said, "Let's make groups of five or six, so we can cover more ground."

Tangtun remembered Nainai saying something similar, that more people make better work.

One group carrying oil lamps and torches started up the hill into the village, and another went through the fields. The third group crossed the road to search gullies and ravines where no one lived. The last headed into the woods.

"I'll stay here," MaMa said, "in case Meimei comes home on her own."

Ba spoke, "Tangtun, two or three of you boys go to all your favourite places near the creek. She's followed you there before. Maybe she went today."

Tangtun and Little Ming dashed into the woods with Haohao lumbering along behind. Crunching over fallen leaves, they headed through the clearing where Tangtun often drew charcoal sketches of doves on rocks. At first no signs of life stirred in the dark silence, but as their eyes adjusted, they began to see more than black stick-like trees. The doves slept with heads under their wings on low limbs of scrub oaks near the edge of the clearing.

"Dumb birds roosting right there," said Haohao in disgust. "They're always pecking our rice plants and getting in my way when I patch the dikes. I'm going to whack them with a stick, so they won't bother me anymore." He grabbed a big branch and headed toward the birds.

"No! You can't!" Tangtun jumped between Haohao and the doves. "My grandmother said doves mate for life and always live in the same place. Even if you chase them off, they'll just settle nearby."

"Hey, forget the birds. Meimei's not here," Little Ming said, "and it's starting to snow."

Turning to run again, Tangtun said, "Let's go to the big rock. She follows me there sometimes." They dodged low limbs and jumped over dead logs. They heard the creek before they saw it. "Meimei, Meimei" they repeated, circling the boulder with Tangtun's fading drawings on it.

"Maybe if we climb on top we can see something," Tangtun started up with Little Ming right behind and Haohao peering all around.

Atop the rock, the wind and snow hit them harder. With hands protecting their eyes, they looked upstream and saw only dark woods and white-tipped water spilling over nearby rocks. The clouds shut out the moon and stars and snow flurried all around them. They turned together to look downstream. Nothing hinted at a little girl passing that way.

Dejected Tangtun and Little Ming slid off the rock and landed beside Haohao.

"Wait!" Tangtun's hand darted out to stop Little Ming. "What is that?"

"Only the water," said Haohao.

"Shssh! Listen!"

They held their breath. Then they heard it, the sound of someone crying far, far away. They looked at each other, cupped hands around their mouths, took a deep breath and yelled together, "Meimei!"

"Tangtun, is that you?" They barely understood the question in the wind.

"It's her, it's her." Little Ming jumped up and down.

"Be quiet." Tangtun strained to hear. He said, "Keep yelling, Meimei, so we can find you. Where are you?"

"Here! I'm here!"

Tangtun ran down the bank, shouting, "This way!"

CHAPTER 30

"Can we count on you?"

The trio jumped from rock to rock, holding on to saplings to keep from falling in the river. Out of breath, they stopped. They heard only the water slapping over rocks.

"Meimei," they yelled again in unison.

"Over here!"

"We passed her," said Little Ming. "She's back up that way."

They scrambled together up the bank and into the trees.

"I'm down here." Meimei's voice sounded a little louder but they still saw nothing.

"Did she say down?" Tangtun stopped to ask. "But she sounds above us."

They climbed up the hillside, over rocks and around bushes, holding on to trees to pull themselves along. Meimei's voice grew louder. With one last heave, they crested the ridge and looked down into a deep crevice. Younger Sister lay against a large snow-spattered rock a long way below them. Her tear-streaked face beamed when she saw them. "I knew you'd find me, Gege."

"Sweet, Older Brother." Haohao couldn't resist making fun.

"Stop, Haohao!"

"We can't reach her," Tangtun whispered to the boys. "Are you hurt?" he said louder to Meimei.

"I hit this rock. It hurts when I breathe."

"Be still, Meimei. We're coming down."

"How?" asked Little Ming.

Tangtun looked all around, then ran toward a tree and began to climb. Stepping on to a limb and sliding out, he crossed his ankles underneath and leaned far to the side until his fingers touched a long hanging vine. "Catch this," he called out. He pulled his knife out of his waist pouch, leaned again to pull the vine toward him and hacked first one way and another making a notch. Then he sawed until the vine fell.

Back on the ground, he ordered. "You two hold the vine like this." He placed them behind each other with gnarly knots in each hand. "Now I'll climb down to get Meimei."

The boys nodded without comment. Tangtun gripped hard to secure his hold and backed toward the edge of the ridge. Little Ming and Haohao braced their feet against rocks.

"Ugh!" Their breath whooshed from their lungs as Tangtun stepped out into the air and bounced back against the rock face and down to Meimei.

"Put your arms around my neck and your legs around my waist, Meimei." She did, biting her lip while tears ran down her face.

"Good girl, now hold on." He tucked one arm under her bottom, while the other, straining under their combined weights, felt like it would come out of his shoulder. "Pull," he screamed to his friends and began to walk up the crevice wall.

As quickly as possible, the boys returned to the house with Tangtun carrying Meimei in his arms. MaMa ran out of the house crying, "You found her, you found her!" She hugged Meimei close. Ba rested his hand on Tangtun's shoulder.

Tangtun heard people calling to one another in every direction, “We’ve found her. She’s safe! Stop looking. Come back now.”

Gathering around the boys, they clamoured to hear the story of how they had found her. Nainai poured tea as they chattered and laughed. A few people ambled off toward their homes, but most stood around in twos and threes enjoying the happy ending.

Later, Tangtun leaned against the wall between Little Ming and Haohao and said, “Nainai says more people make better work. Haohao, it’s good you are so big.”

“True,” Little Ming nodded. “I could not have held that vine without help.”

Haohao shrugged. “It was nothing.” He shifted straighter and added, “The coldest part of night had not come yet and your sister was shivering already. We needed everyone searching to find her.”

Tangtun bumped Little Ming’s hip. “Maybe the searchers can save us, too, help us finish the bells on time.”

He slid among the people to Nainai and told her his idea. “Talk to your father,” she said.

When Tangtun found Ba with Haohao’s uncle and told them, Ba didn’t respond, only frowned with a far-away look in his eye.

Haohao’s uncle squeezed Ba’s shoulder and said, “I think Tangtun should tell everyone his idea.”

Tangtun’s mouth dropped open. Then Ba clapped his hands for everyone’s attention and Tangtun jumped.

Ba cleared his throat. ”I want to say….”

He paused and began again. "My family is filled with gratitude tonight for the safety of our child, and for you …"

He shook his head, swallowed, and finished in a whisper, "*Du li nan zhi*. One alone is not strong enough."

The silence in the room ached.

Haohao's uncle coughed and said, "Tangtun wants to talk."

Everyone shifted and looked at Tangtun. Taking a deep breath, he said, "We cannot finish the bells in time for the wedding."

"What?" someone said, "But then…"

"Then we'll lose our jobs, and…" Tangtun dropped his voice, "…the whole village might starve." Everyone stared back at him, stunned that he described their situation so plainly. "And the king kills BaBa and me."

The silence could not have been louder.

"No one's going to die," Nainai said. "We're all willing to help, but old people can't work in the foundry." Nods of agreement circled the room.

"And I'm too little," piped up Meimei from MaMa's lap.

"The younger boys can join us apprentices," said Tangtun. "And, all of us can work longer hours if someone brings evening meals to us. And, we need bell players, hammers and sticks for the players. Who has ideas about how we can move the bells? They're heavy. I'm sure each of you can do something the same way you did tonight."

With those few words, Tangtun tapped into the warmth of their shared success in finding a lost child and the concern for their common need. Everyone started talking at once, eager to decide how to help save their village.

Tangtun looked around the room and then back at Ba's sombre face, "We can count on them, BaBa."

CHAPTER 31

In the snow-covered foundry, everyone scurried between coppersmith Red's fire and the furnaces, warming themselves before moving back to colder work spots. Relieved that more helpers had sped up the bell-making, Tangtun shrugged his shoulders and rolled his head, trying to shake the uneasiness that nagged him like a toothache.

The extra help would quicken the long, tedious process of lacquering the rack parts. Earlier in the summer, workers had collected the yellow sap from the lac trees, then filtered it of impurities and heated it to remove the water from it. MaMa had added cinnabar to colour it red and stored it.

"We need to keep Haohao away from the lacquer," he reminded Little Ming.

Men and boys dipped the hundreds of wooden pieces in the lacquer, leaving it to harden in the humid air, and then dipping it again. The script writer carved characters into the hard, middle layer of lacquer, the metal worker tapped gold into them after which they would be covered with lighter lacquer. The waiting for each layer to harden made it a slow, slow process. Everyone wondered when the final layer would be added.

Tangtun feared the worst. Haohao, of course, spoke it. "Old Bear breathes freezing air. My hands, ears, even my nose is numb. We can't finish by the first spring moon."

"Say it again, and faster, Haohao," Little Ming said. "Maybe more words can warm you."

Stamping his feet, Tangtun didn't laugh. The threat of death dragged him awake every morning and stalked him through each day. "The bells aren't finished. Even the Master says he's having trouble writing a song that is good enough. And, when he does, who can play it?" He constantly worried out loud with Little Ming.

Heavy-hearted with dread of failure and afraid BaBa and he would both die, Tangtun headed for his favourite place, the woods. In the gathering dusk, he plopped down on a snow-dusted tree root, stuck his freezing hands inside his sleeves and gripped his elbows. He hunkered down with his shoulders drawn up to his ears and stared at a lean gray dove pecking under shrubs, eating stray pine nuts and seeds. She made a low throaty sound and with a whistle of wings and an answering warble her mate joined her.

At first their cooing sounded sad like they had lost something, but soon repetition of the two soft notes became hypnotic. He leaned against the trunk of the chestnut tree and stared at the deserted twig, grass, and pine needle nest the pair had built together in the spring in the crotch of a tree at field's edge.

Tangtun's mind wandered. My parents want me to be like a dove. BaBa wants me to have a family and provide for them when I grow up. "Huh," he grunted. No bells, no more worries about any of that.

He sighed and poked with a stick at acorns in the dried leaves. "I should take these to MaMa to cook," he murmured. It's hard to imagine having a wife, even harder a life without art.

BaBa probably won't enjoy his surprise I'm working on every day.

He brushed a spot clear and drew a house with a man and his family. He tilted his head thinking, who am I really?

Then the doves' cooing answered him, one note, soft, loud and a second short one repeated low three times, Ooo-OOH, Ooo, Ooo, Ooo. They're talking. He began to coo himself, first pretending to be BaBa dove and then MaMa dove. Then he pitched his voice higher and made a light fragile pair of coo sounds. Soon he was cooing from high to low, up and down, as far ranging as his voice could go.

Suddenly he laughed out loud and the doves scooted for cover. What if the bells played two tunes in some kind of pattern, like doves talking? Pushing up from the tree, he slapped snow off his pants and said to the pair of birds, "Thank you! I'm going to tell Master Musician."

Pulling his winter tunic tight around his neck and ducking his head into the wind, he cut through the darkening woods heading uphill. He moved fast, hoping to get home before MaMa gathered search teams the way BaBa and he had done for Meimei.

At the Master's house, he pushed the door open. "It's Tangtun. May I come in?"

The tall, white-haired musician laughed. "You're in. Come, sit here by the stove."

Tangtun explained his dove music idea. "Can you write a wedding song that sounds like two people talking?" he asked.

Master stroked his long white beard. "Tangtun, bells have always made two sounds, so that should work well with your idea. We'll have a song to celebrate the union of two kingdoms and two people."

"Two kingdoms, two persons, so maybe two songs?"

"Good idea! Now, how can I do that?"

He began to think out loud. "Hmm … the Double Circle of Life … two lives united … take flight together."

Tangtun dared not speak.

Master stood with one arm lifting and fingers flipping through the air and the other following underneath as he spoke to himself, "The female, light and beautiful, flies high. The male, heavy and undergirding, supports. One tune ascends while the other descends, going round and round from the cry of birth to the silence of death…" And, so, forgetting Tangtun, he moved over to his desk under the window, picked up his short *dizi* and began to play a high-pitched melody.

Tangtun slipped out of the door and hurried home. In the dim shaft of light from the open door, his parents stood a few feet apart, an arguing distance he knew well.

"Tangtun," his mother said as he stepped into the yard. The bottom of his stomach dropped to his feet.

"I had something to do, MaMa."

"So your father said." She frowned at Ba. "I wanted the neighbours to look for you, but he said no." She turned and walked into the house.

Ba watched her walk away. "I said wait, to give you some time. Now come inside and tell us where you were."

Relieved they hadn't gone looking for him and puzzled by his father's calm tone, Tangtun followed them inside. He stood in the middle of the floor with eyes glowing, telling them about wedding songs.

"Good ideas, Tangtun," his mother said. Tangtun smiled.

"Hmm," said his father. "Let's wait for what Master writes, before we get too excited about this."

Dropping his head, Tangtun went to bed. He squared his jaw and whispered to himself, "You'll see, Ba, you'll see."

CHAPTER 32

The next night in Nainai's room with Tangtun's paintings of morning glory vines and birds trailing across the walls, Tangtun bent over his leaf drawing. His left arm curled around the leaf, so he wouldn't smear the wet dye as he drew his secret creation for BaBa with his left hand.

"Who is smart enough to play the bells, Nainai?"

"Most girls in the village enjoy making music with sticks. They hit clay, wood, anything. They could probably do it."

Tangtun sighed, thinking, girls don't play bells. Only the Master does. Aloud he said, "You're right. They could practice the rhythm with sticks, tapping on blocks, even clay mold pieces."

He drew some more and added, "Maybe the Master could teach them to hum their notes along with his *dizi* and hit the chime stones to teach them some sounds of the bigger bells."

Nainai nodded as she stirred her evening meal, "Trust me. By the time the bells are finished, they'll be ready to play the songs on them, too."

"Hmm, I'm not sure girls are that smart."

Nainai turned to stare at him. "If Little Ming and you can master swords, girls can master playing songs."

Tangtun grinned at her. "Well, we work at it," he said. "Maybe girls can work hard, too."

At the foundry the cold short days covered with clouds dragged by with rain and sometimes snow adding misery to the monotony.

"When is spring coming?" Haohao complained.

Tangtun said, "Not before we're ready, I hope."

Then, Master Musician finished the wedding music and, just as Nainai had said, Tangtun found village girls eager to play it. Three tall girls agreed to stand behind the rack to strike with hammers their assigned sections of the middle tier and the smallest bells at arms' length above their heads. One more would manage the bells on the shorter side of the rack. The oldest girl accepted the out-front responsibility for the large bells near the floor. She would use a heavy stick to make the big bells ring.

Meimei begged to be a player, too. "I want to play, too. Let me, let me."

"Try then," said Tangtun. He hung some small bells on a tree limb and handed her a T-shaped hammer. She almost dropped it.

"Careful. This hammer is heavy and a third your height. To play the bells, you must be able to hold it above your head."

Meimei gripped it with both hands and brought it over her head. Its weight pulled it down against her back. Bracing herself on one leg, she yelled "Ah-h-h!" and tried to bring it forward over her head. The hammer flew sideways, out of her grip, and she fell, tumbling over and over. Sitting up on her hands, she looked at Tangtun and cried, "It's too big!"

"Yes, it is, Meimei," he said pulling her to her feet. "We'll find something else for you."

Day after day the players all joined the Master Musician at his home. First they memorised the melody by listening to the Master hum phrases, play them on his *dizi* or chime stones, and repeating them as best they could on the small set of village bells.

Soon the Master took them to the foundry where finished bells lay on the ground in groups according to size and pitch with empty spaces for some not yet made. Everyone grimaced at the strange sounds the girls made, when hitting grounded bells that were supposed to be hung and humming and thudding down on the place of missing ones. No one had another plan, so they listened in silence and hoped the girls succeeded.

When the girls got tired, Tangtun said, "You girls sound great." Little Ming danced a jig and they giggled.

"That pounding on the ground hurts my ears," Haohao complained. "We're all doomed." Every time he did, someone said, "Trust the Master. He knows what he is doing."

Others said, "Quiet, Haohao," or ,"Remember, *du li nan zhi*. One person alone is not strong enough."

Then the last winter moon went to its heavenly palace and slept longer than any other night of the year. The darkness dampened the spirits of everyone, making their hands slower and their feet drag even more from job to job.

After a few days, a sliver of light appeared in the early evening sky.

"The moon is waking up," said Master Musician, "and the Great Bear's tail soon turns toward the home of the morning sun.

When the moon refuses to shine two more times, Fang Festival and the wedding happen at the same time. The bells must be ready, or else."

CHAPTER 33

Soon sunny days began to outnumber the cold, wintry ones. Large white cranes returned north above the spring-green growth of the trees. Tangtun watched mother ducks, with their ducklings, waddle in a line, along the riverbank where long-legged herons tiptoed.

Fang Festival is just weeks away. We are not going to finish the bells in time.

One afternoon the sunshine gave way to a peculiar yellow light as heavy, black clouds advanced across the Jiangshan Plain. The stillness and quiet of trees and birds made Tangtun's skin crawl along the back of his neck, chill behind his ears, and tighten on his scalp.

Like an unnamed danger, the storm crept closer. The wind blew harder until fat drops of rain splattered on leaves and ground and sped up to a maddening pace. Tangtun dashed for cover, knowing the rainy season had arrived early in the land of Jingnan. Yet his head drooped more from the shortness of time than the wet.

For four days the rain fell with no break. Thunder rolled across the marsh and ricocheted among the hills. It sounded as if the gods intended to drum the earth to death. The mountains disappeared behind a shroud of gray rain and puddles around the house grew wide and deep.

Work at the foundry slowed and everyone sloshed around in the puddles. Rain running through their hair and dripping off their noses pulled their faces and spirits down even more.

"Mud squishing between my toes feels good," Tangtun said, trying to cheer up Little Ming. They loaded a wheelbarrow with rocks and then together pushed it in a wobbling, curving path through the foundry.

Little Ming's mouth barely lifted at the edges. "It sucks in my whole foot and steals my shoes," he said.

Soon water snaked through the foundry, licking at little discards of daily life—wood bits, coal chips, broken baskets—and drawing them along with it. Even clay molds began to float. Outdoor work at the foundry came to a halt. Idle workers gathered along the river bank to watch the rising waters. Worried neighbours considered moving to higher ground.

The incessant rain drove all families indoors and the whole world dripped. Sitting cross-legged on the bed between MaMa and Meimei, Tangtun felt imprisoned by the rain and the dampness of everything. His skin sweated, his clothes clung, soggy hair drooped in his eyes, the skin on his toes wrinkled.

I. Hate. Rain.

Just then, Ba ducked in the door along with a clap of thunder.

"The creek is way out of its banks," he said, "and the river is rising fast. We have to go to higher ground. Tangtun, get Nainai out!"

Tangtun jumped to obey.

In her room at the back of the house, Nainai scrambled about, putting clothes in a basket on top of her low-lying bed where she had been napping. She tried to lift her small table up beside the clothes.

"There's no time, Nainai," yelled Tangtun. "Come with me!"

He splashed over to her and caught her arm. "We must go up the mountain."

They stepped outside into moving water and struggled toward higher ground, dodging floating branches. Mysterious underwater slaps and brushes against their legs made them step higher and twist away.

Tangtun eyed snakes riding the knee-high current just beyond arms reach. What if one coils around me—or bites me?

"Stop worrying about snakes," Grandmother said. "They want to be safe as much as we do."

Soon Tangtun felt Nainai bouncing up and down on her toes to keep her head above the rising water. Without warning she lost her footing and went under. Tangtun grabbed her arm, pulled her up and held her tight against his side. Breathing hard, he swung his other arm out for balance. He wobbled left and then right, his feet searching for solid ground. He stepped once, twice, but the third time onto nothing. They both went down and he felt Nainai slip from his grasp.

"No," he screamed. Water poured into his mouth, choking him. He shot up into the air, coughing and looking through sheets of rain in every direction for her. He saw only the angry river, jumping up the walls of the houses, splatting down and disappearing across the yard into the woods and darkness.

I've lost her, I've lost her. Where did she go?

Spinning in a crooked circle, he saw no sign of her. "Nainai, Nainai," he said. He lost his balance and felt himself sucked into a whirlpool, crushed down by the water monster, alive and determined to hold him under. Twisting and turning against the weight, Tangtun forced his feet straight downward and his arms upward, rocketing himself gasping into the air.

Then, he saw Nainai's head, bobbing just ahead of him, and lunged forward. Catching her tunic when he shot by her, he held tight while his momentum carried them both into the low-hanging branches of a tree. Throwing an arm over a branch, he asked, "Nainai, Nainai, are you alright?"

Coughing and spitting water, she managed a weak smile. "Yes, Tangtun, I'm safe—because of you."

Tangtun closed his eyes and held her close. I did it. I saved her. To Nainai he simply said, "It was nothing."

With new confidence he pulled her with him to the next tree and the next, then up the path to the top of the hill. His family and neighbours huddled there in stunned silence, staring at the flood waters and trying not to think of their losses. MaMa drew Nainai and him close saying, "Nainai, Tangtun," while Ba stood with them in silence.

Tangtun allowed the embrace, nodded and then stared downhill, dripping from head to toe and wishing he could see a bell. He said to no one in particular, "What else can possibly happen to us?"

Ba began to give orders. The men tied long tree branches against big trees, and Tangtun and the other apprentices gathered short branches to lay over them. With no food and nothing to do, everyone crawled underneath the lean-to shelters and lay shivering, listening to the rain, and longing for morning light.

CHAPTER 34

When they awoke, the rain had stopped and the water had begun to drain down from the village toward the foundry and river.

Tangtun asked, "BaBa, do you think our bells are still there?"

"Can't tell until the water leaves the foundry," said Ba. "Let's right the village first."

Tangtun surveyed the damage with all the villagers. Pots and pans, tables and stools lay all awry where swirling waters had tossed them. The sour stench of river mud and dying fish filled the air. He blinked away tears.

"The river god dumped mud ankle-deep in every house. How can anything survive?"

Tangtun and Little Ming worked alongside the other villagers, shovelling dirt and debris, picking up household items, washing and re-washing them, but nothing could get all the sticky mud off. Even Haohao without a complaint helped drape clothes on bushes and spread wet rice on rocks to dry in the sunlight.

In the bottom of a rice basket filled with mud and rocks, Tangtun saw a familiar tail sticking up and pulled. "Meimei," he yelled. "Here's your lost tiger!"

Meimei came running and laughing. "Oh, oh, oh!" Hugging the toy close, she whispered, "Hello, Tiger, I'm glad Elder Brother found you. Then she ran off toward the village hemp shop, singing out, "MaMa! Look, look!"

"Hope that helps MaMa," Tangtun said to his friends, digging again.

Little Ming said, "Me, too. She hasn't smiled since she discovered all her precious dyes gone with the water."

That night the villagers all fell exhausted onto damp mats outdoors as the chickens roosted on low tree branches. The next day Tangtun, Ba and other workers slogged their way to the foundry.

"Hey, I see something shiny!" shouted Little Ming.

"It's the hangers on the rack beams," said Tangtun beginning to run. "They're sticking out of the mud."

Others began to run and shout, too.

"I see a warrior post!"

"There's another one!"

"Here's another and another! They were too heavy to float away!"

Hope drove the men and boys. Closer in they saw the edges of the largest bells turned over but still there.

"Let's dig them out," Tangtun said.

Ba said. "You boys start digging. Men, let's search for more bells."

The apprentices attacked the disarray. Each bell they uncovered brought a shout, "Here's one!" Soon they spread out three lines of bells in their hanging order, leaving spaces for the missing ones. Wet and muddy, they finally collapsed on the ground around the bells. More than one eye glistened with unshed tears in people both happy and sad.

"Too many bells were carried away by the river," said one worker.

"Or they're buried under all that mud," said another. "We'll probably never find them."

"We still have to finish the set while we remake the lost ones." The worker who had been counting the bells slapped his wet thigh. "That's only a third of the bells, and all the hammers and long sticks have disappeared as well."

"Cleaning and drying these rack beams can be a time-eating task, too," said another.

Ba added, "Time we don't have. The new moon has already come out of its heavenly palace. Twenty-eight days won't be enough."

"Then the sooner we start the better," Tangtun said. "Meanwhile, BaBa, can you send King Wang a message about the flood and lost bells. Maybe he'll take a smaller set."

Ba nodded and motioned everyone to get moving.

With leaden steps, they began to get the foundry in working order again. They worried about what the king might say. "If we don't obey his order for sixty-four bells, Ba and Tangtun die," they talked in low voices among themselves. "What can we do, what can we do?"

CHAPTER 35

Together we win!

Thubalup, thubalup, thubalup! The king's personal envoy galloped into the middle of the foundry. Drawn up short, his horse danced around, knocking Little Ming and Haohao off their feet. Little Ming's cart toppled and coal tumbled everywhere. Without dismounting, the envoy spoke in a loud voice, "Workers of Jingnan, come! Hear the message of your king, Mighty King Wang."

Silent men with stone faces surrounded him. Then he read in terrible thundering tones.

"Jianjun's request is denied. The marriage of Chu and Zeng," he read, clearing his throat, "the marriage will happen as scheduled! In twenty-six days, at the Festival of Fang, the Jingnan Foundry will play the complete set of *bianzhong*, the gift of King Wang to Marquis Yi. You will not present a smaller bell set. No one dishonours the king of Chu and lives. Deliver the sixty-four bells as promised and on time, or ..."

He paused and the breath went out of all the people listening. Then he lifted both arms, higher with each pronouncement. "...Or, or, you Jianjun, your son Tangtun there, and every man and boy of this foundry pays with his life. Your ears will be cut off, then your hands and feet, and finally your heads. You will die a slow death!"

"No!" Ba stepped toward the soldier, who yelled, "Hear the word of Wang, King of the Chu!" He spun his rearing horse, kicked his heels in its side, and galloped away.

The words echoed through the foundry as everyone froze in horror. When they looked at Ba for help, he bowed his head and trudged out, climbing slowly up the path toward the village. Tangtun followed him at a distance.

At the house, Tangtun stopped just outside the door and peeked in. He watched and listened to his parents talk in low tones on their bed.

"I can't do it, Lin," Ba cried. "I can't have the death of my only son, and all the other workers and their sons, on my head."

Seeing his mother draw his slumped father into her arms, Tangtun walked away. He strode around the house to the shed. Climbing on a stool, he stretched up to the roof where he had hidden his treasure box from Meimei. His fingers found it, still damp. Pulling it loose, he squatted atop the stool and forced open the stuck lid.

He pondered his prized piece of artwork lying dry on top.

Is now the time to give this to BaBa? What if he throws it back at me?

He stared deep into the box as if he could see his future. Then he stepped off the stool. Squaring his shoulders, he carried the box back to the front of the house. When he entered, his parents looked up.

"BaBa, I made this for you."

Ba opened the box and drew out a leaf with no green left on it, only veins ribbed its thin, cloudy membrane. The light from the open doorway shone through it, lighting up the image of a man.

"You drew a soldier?" asked his mother.

"I drew BaBa, the soldier," Tangtun said, tensing for another rejection, but rushing on. "Once you were a fine swordsman, a brave warrior. Now, you'll fight again, fight to finish the bells, fight against time. You'll protect us all from King Wang. I know you can."

BaBa looked at the leaf, then at Tangtun, and back at the leaf. He placed it with care in the box, stood up and said, "Again you remind me of my own words, *du li nan zhi*. One alone is not strong enough."

Ba headed for the door, saying, "Come on, my son. You and I have a job to finish."

Tangtun flushed with warmth, thinking, *Yes! The old BaBa is back!*

CHAPTER 36

At the foundry, Tangtun and Ba moved side by side as twin dynamos, assigning workers to each step of the bell-making process. They helped until they glistened with sweat, stopping only to swig water and swallow a few bites of cold rice. One by one, the workers' fear and despair changed to determination. Everyone began working faster and harder, following the example of their two leaders.

Each evening Tangtun watched the sun dip below the distant hills and flood the sky with orange fading to baby pink. As light purple deepened to dark blue and the moon rose in the night sky, he counted the number of new bells finished that day. After two weeks, every inch of his tired body knew.

We cannot finish in time. We need more help.

Instead of going home that night, he went from house to house using the same arguments he had used with his father to persuade the last villagers, the oldest and the youngest to help.

"We are fighters," he said to the girls. To the small boys, he bragged, "We never quit!"

"Help us, so not a single villager dies," he begged the elderly.

"In a few days, this full moon disappears," he told the women, "and the wedding day arrives."

Without hesitation, the rest of the villagers followed him to the foundry. They worked by moonlight and torchlight that night, and the night after that, and then another, and another.

Not only did they remake bells, they also prepared ways to transport them. Little Ming and Big Ming recruited two farmers with waggons for the long, heavy warrior posts. Other villagers brought carts, lined them up ready for the medium-sized bells. Three fishermen tied their boats up at the riverbank to carry seven heavier bells. Boys and girls gathered bamboo in the daytime and at night helped the men lash it with hemp ropes into two rafts to carry the four biggest bells up river. The elders cut long strips of bamboo and soaked them in water. Then they braided them into strong ropes for river trackers to help pull the rafts upstream. Poles of bamboo waited for the women to carry the smaller bells across their shoulders.

And, in the midst of it all, Ba forgot the sword lessons. Tangtun told Little Ming, "Don't worry. We'll learn later."

Night after night Tangtun counted more bell replacements and watched the moon's fullness fading. His neighbours, men, women and children, worked in shifts. A few stopped to prepare food for the rest and then hurried back to work. Some workers napped for a while on mats rolled out wherever they found a spot and then got up and went to work again.

And, finishing the racks for the bells a second time irritated everyone. Some villagers cleaned and re-cleaned the sticky mud off the almost life-sized bronze warrior end posts. Others washed and laid the inscribed beams in the sun to dry. Then they began the tedious task of adding the final layers of waterproof lacquer. They also replaced wooden sticks and large and small hammers for the bell players with new lacquered ones. Haohao was no help, because he had to stay far away from the lacquer.

The moon began its last week as a mere sliver of itself. The whole village wore worry as a heavy shroud, while a few people voiced concerns aloud, "Have you ever seen anyone cut up?"

"I can't imagine dying like that."

Tangtun silenced them. "Stop, think only about your work. Move as fast as possible. We can do this." He never mentioned the fear gnawing at him without let-up. Will King Wang follow through on his threat to kill everyone? Gritting his teeth to still his shakiness, he vowed, No, I won't let that happen.

With the moon growing dimmer, Haohao found dozens of new ways to complain, rotating from one gripe to the other.

"Whose idea was doing lacquer anyway?"

"Those bells hurt my ears!"

"Can't you hurry it up?"

No one bothered to answer him anymore.

Finally, when the moon refused to come out at all, the last bell was finished and laid with the rest. The lacquer of the rack had to be hard, too. Everyone gathered around Tangtun as he tested the top layer of lacquer on the beams. He laid his fingers on it several times in different places.

"It's still tacky. It needs days more to harden before we can move it." Little Ming exhaled a big, breathy sigh and with almost a tear in his eye said slowly, "That means we can't get the bells to tomorrow's wedding on time."

"Are you sure?" Haohao challenged from the back of the crowd while other workers silently dropped their heads in utter defeat. Some sat down on the ground, so tired they could no longer hold themselves up. A few just started walking away.

CHAPTER 37

And then, above the pall that settled over everyone like a blanket, Tangtun shouted. “Little Ming’s teasing. The lacquer is hard.”

Little Ming grinned and punched Tangtun, “I told you we could fool them.”

“What?” Big Ming and Ba spoke at the same time.

“I could kill you myself,” said Haohao laughing, “if I weren’t so happy the rack is ready. Let’s see if it all fits.”

Then, everyone laughed and cheered with him. Several men grabbed each large beam and with Ba calling, “Ready, set, lift,” they pushed them into the bronze warrior end posts. They secured the small racks on top of the large L-shaped hanging rack. Everything fitted perfectly.

Little Ming ran around the racks yelling. “Look how big it is!”

Tangtun said, “It’s almost twice as tall as BaBa.” He ran his hands across the muscular bronze warriors with swords. These even look like BaBa. He put his arm around one and stood on its bronze foot pad, big as a river boulder. He lifted his arms, as if he too were holding up the heavy cross beams.

“These racks dwarf any used with our village instruments,” he said to Little Ming in almost a whisper of reverence. “Look at the black and red colours and gold writing. It’s more impressive than anything—even without the bells on it.”

Just then Ba raised his voice. "No time to stand around admiring. Take that rack apart. Load all the pieces and the bells. We have to get to the palace by midday tomorrow, or else…"

"But we need to practice the wedding songs first with the bells hanging on the rack." The girls all talked at once. "And we've never practiced with the chime stones."

Ba said, "Don't worry. Master Musician knows the chime stones and you girls know your tunes. You've played the bells hanging from tree limbs and waggons."

"But the big ones on the ground just went thud, thud," argued Haohao. "They need to play all the bells on the rack."

"We don't have time, Haohao," said Tangtun, wishing he never had to hear his griping again.

"What if the rack bends from the weight of the bells," said Little Ming, "like an old, bow-backed buffalo?" He dropped his hands to the ground and lumbered around with his back bowed.

Ba raised his arms for silence. "The rack can hold the bells," he promised.

"And, the girls can play the songs without a mistake," said the Master Musician.

"Yes," agreed Tangtun. "It's time to load and move out."

But, deep in his heart, he ached with dread. He whispered to Little Ming, "What if we're late? What if the king sees BaBa and goes into a murderous rage?"

Little Ming looked back with the same fear on his face.

CHAPTER 38

In the darkness, no one stood still. Ba issued orders. "Tangtun, you and the other apprentices help Big Ming put the rafts and boats in the water. Farmer friends, hitch your horses to your waggons and hold them still."

Pointing with his open hand, he continued. "You, you, you, and you, lift the four biggest bells and these ropes onto these two waggons and take them to the rafts. Then come back for the other seven large bells. Put a heavy bell and a lighter one in the first boat, same in the second boat, and the last three into the third boat. When a boat is ready, you start downriver."

"Carpenter, direct these remaining men and boys to take apart the bell rack and load the warrior posts and beams onto the waggons when they arrive back from the river. Then get those horses headed toward Ying."

"Everyone else divide the thirty-three middle-sized bells among these three carts. The water buffalo are ready, so you can drive as soon as you are loaded."

Turning to the Master Musician he said, "I trust you to move all these waggons and people through the night to arrive at Ying before the wedding. When you arrive, set up the rack and hang the bells you carry." The Master dropped his head in a slight bow.

"Wait a moment." Ba swiftly walked to his workbench and back. "Keep these safe for us," he said, handing Tangtun's and his swords to the Master, "until our boats and rafts meet you at Ying."

Meanwhile, MaMa directed the women and girls. "Ladies, here are nine bamboo rods. Hang a bell on each end and tie it with hemp. That should keep your bells from falling off your rods on our long walk."

"I want one," said Meimei, jumping up and down.

"You're too little," said Tangtun but stopped when he saw MaMa frown.

"Yes, Meimei," MaMa said. "We'll have one bell left over, a bell that is just your size."

Tangtun said. "And, I'll help find a rod to fit you." Digging through some scraps, he soon discovered a bamboo pole just her size. The smile on Younger Sister's face made him feel good all over.

"Girls," MaMa continued. "You can each carry your own hammer or stick, but first, run home to get your festival dresses for the wedding." She clapped her hands. "Hurry now."

Master Musician sat tall on the first waggon heading out. As each loaded waggon, cart, and person followed, villager after villager scanned the sky for rain. With the moon asleep in its heavenly palace for the second night, they carried burning torches to light their way to Ying.

Tangtun pictured the next day, Fang Festival Day. Happy crowds enjoying a celebration—IF we get the bells there before the sun stands high overhead and the wedding begins. He turned toward the river and the rafts, shaking off the shiver of fear that ran down his spine and declared out loud, "Not if! When!"

CHAPTER 39

The rafts holding the four heaviest bells headed down the Great River toward the mouth of the stream they would follow to Ying. Tangtun and Ba poled one raft and Little Ming and his father poled the other. Each father and son team pushed their raft close to the bank to avoid the strong centre current.

In the darkness, Tangtun strained to see ahead.

We have to get there in time, we have to.

A light rain began to fall and the torch on the raft sputtered and smoked, giving only a faint light. He said, "Ba, do you think MaMa and everyone can get to Ying without breaking down in the mud?"

Ba shoved hard with his pole. "They must," he grunted with another thrust of his pole. "We can't help them. We're turning upstream—right now."

Tangtun saw no stream, but the strong current from the left whirled them out toward the middle of the Great River. "Push, Tangtun," Ba yelled. "Stay in control or we'll spin around and go down river for miles!"

Tangtun leaned harder on his pole to stabilize the rear of the raft while Ba angled his pole to turn it up into the smaller stream. Water splashed all over them, wetting them from head to toe. Tangtun spit and shook his hair out of his face like a wet dog and kept pushing. They made the turn, but the rain-swelled current rushing downstream threatened to reverse their course.

“Look there. It’s our river trackers,” shouted Ba as he spotted wiry workmen lining the tiny path notched into the cliff wall. “Throw the rope to them, Tangtun.”

Tangtun laid down his pole, snatched up the coiled main rope whose split ends had been tied fast around a post on each corner of the front of the raft. Then he leaned back and threw the coil as hard as he could toward the trackers on the bank. Just downstream Little Ming’s rope snaked through the air at the same time.

Each tracker looped a split section of rope over his shoulder to lie across his back as he gripped the main rope and trudged along the left bank. As one, the four men bowed under the strain of pulling the raft upstream while keeping it out of the strong middle current. Little Ming’s raft followed close behind.

As the current strengthened, the river trackers began to make loud sounds. “Hey hum, ho hoo-oom. Hey la da so wa-a-ah!”

“What’s that?” Tangtun yelled.

Ba chuckled. “They’re singing. It’s not pretty, but it keeps them together and helps them forget how tired they are.”

“Then let’s join them!” Tangtun said.

Soon everyone sang to the rhythm of their work, but without a moon and with clouds hiding the stars, they had no idea how much time they had left. And rapids lay just ahead.

***

Meanwhile on the road, the caravan of villagers bowed under the rain and kept slogging along beside the waggons and carts. “Oh! No-o-o-o,” screamed Meimei and Nainai from the rear.

Everyone spun to see the last waggon tilting at an odd angle and bells tumbling out. The driver slapped the reins against the horses, "Pull! Pull!"

Master Musician said, "It's stuck! Haohao, put something solid under that wheel!"

Haohao jumped down. The walkers dropped their loads. All scrambled to find branches and rocks. Haohao lifted the back end while others threw things under the wheel. The driver shouted, "Go, go," at the horses and they strained to pull the waggon. As the waggon lurched forward, the branches broke and the wheel sank even deeper into the mud.

"More rocks and branches," said Haohao, straining to hold up the waggon for the workers to throw rocks and twigs beneath the wheel. Soon they created a firm spot for the wheel to drop back on. With one final shout from the driver, "Pull!" the horses lunged forward and the waggon popped out on the road again.

"Hoo! Yeh!" everyone shouted and smiled and nodded at Haohao. Then they worked together to reload the bells.

"Shoulder your bells," said MaMa to the ladies, "and walk faster. We have to make up for lost time."

The caravan didn't stop again. The night grew longer and their legs more tired. When the rain let up, they passed around buns and water and chewed while trudging on. Finally, Meimei sat down and cried. "I'm sleepy. I'm tired," she blubbered, "and my bell is too heavy."

Haohao said, "Crybaby!"

"Hush, now," Nainai told him. She reached for Meimei's bell and added it to her rod.

Another woman said to MaMa, "I'll take your rod. You carry your daughter."

And so they shared their burdens through the long night.

Just before daylight, Nainai pointed behind them at the four lights of Fang low in the sky. She said, "The celestial horses ride the sky. Today is time for Fang Festival and the noontime Royal Wedding."

No one responded. They walked slowly on with heavy steps, glad for more light, but unsure of the distance to the city or if they would be there in time.

Then someone yelled, "Look! Isn't that smoke?"

"Yes," said another. "It's lots of smoke. What's burning?"

"It's from cooking fires in the city. Ying is waking up," Master said loudly.

"We're almost there!" said someone else.

"Hurry!" said MaMa. "We have to get there and unload in time to meet the boats."

With the end in sight, new resolve empowered everyone's tired feet.

CHAPTER 40

"We. Are. Dead."

Back on the water, Tangtun poled his raft against the current and ignored his aching muscles. The trackers had worked in tandem to pull them safely through the rapids, so now the current seemed less threatening.

As the sun peeked over the hills and made the river sparkle, he smiled at fish jumping and birds diving for breakfast. The boats were out of sight around the bend ahead of the rafts.

"Ying is just ahead," said Little Ming from the trailing raft.

"And we are arriving on time," Tangtun yelled back with a big smile.

Then a tracker tripped. He fell into his partner and lost his grip on the rope to Tangtun's raft. It lurched right and started to turn, ramming into Little Ming's raft before breaking up. Bamboo pieces flew everywhere while Tangtun, Ba, and one bell dropped into the water. Tangtun instinctively grabbed at the bell, hooked a finger through its hanger loop and tumbled with it. He rode the bell downward until they both landed against a boulder on the river bottom. He turned, kicked off the rock with his feet, and shot out of the water, coughing and spitting.

"BaBa!" He spun around, looking in every direction. He saw the other raft passing by out in the river and heard his father yelling to their trackers, "Tie your end of the rope to a tree."

"Here, Tangtun," yelled Ba, swimming toward him holding up the other rope end. "We have to find the bell and tie this through the hanger."

"It's against a rock right here," Tangtun said, taking the rope and diving. When he felt the river bottom, the bell wasn't there.

He looked around but the cloudy water hid everything. He felt for it until he could no longer breathe. Surfacing he gulped a lung full of air and dove again. He reached and kicked in every direction, hoping to touch the bell, but found nothing. Up he went again, popping out of the water.

Ba saw the rope still in his hand and yelled. "We're floating downstream from where we crashed."

Tangtun turned upstream, struggling to make headway, and finally diving again. At the bottom he bumped into the bell and the boulder. Quickly he pushed the rope through the bell hanger loop and resurfaced, yelling, "Got it!" He swam to shore and joined the trackers pulling on the rope. Like a game of tug-of-war with the monster river, the six of them pulled and grunted, pulled and grunted until the bell landed on the bank of the river, kerplunk, thud. All collapsed beside it.

Sucking in air, Tangtun stared at the cloudy sky overhead, his body heavy with fatigue. We will never make it now.

He lifted only his head and saw BaBa up and waving Little Ming's raft away from the bank and on toward the city barely visible in the distance. Their four dejected trackers lay with eyes closed, breathing hard.

Jumping up, Tangtun shouted, "Run! Catch the floating bamboo pieces."

Jarred from their stupor, some trackers took off downstream to get ahead of the floating wood. Several jumped in and began to grab bamboo, holding pieces under one arm until they had no more room, then swimming for shore.

Tangtun turned to Ba, "We can mend the raft, but we need more rope."

"See those trees we passed earlier. You men run downstream, pull off the vines and braid them," Ba said.

The trackers ran. They pulled and braided like demons and passed vine ropes to other men steadying the surviving part of the raft half in the water. One bell still perched on it. Ba and Tangtun raced to tie bamboo pieces with the vine rope in crazy broken patterns. Tangtun wished for his knife, but it had floated away, too.

The raft began to level out and float again. The sun inched toward its highest point in the sky, ready to pour down springtime blessings on the happy newlyweds and rulers.

"We've almost got it," said Tangtun.

Then over the rush of the river, they heard the low continuous rumble of a large gong being struck repeatedly. Bong! Bong! Bong!

"The marriage is announced," said Ba.

"We. Are. Dead," said Tangtun.

"No," said Ba. "The wedding banquet has just begun. It will go on for hours. And, unless they had trouble on the road, the others have the rack and their bells in place by now."

"Then we can get there in time," Tangtun said, "hurry."

"We're braiding as fast as we can," a tracker said.

"This is the last of the bamboo," Ba said. He grabbed a piece, lashed it into place and moved on to draw the next piece up to the raft.

Finally, Tangtun helped some men push the bell while Ba and another steadied the raft. With one mighty "Heave!" they lifted it up and onto the raft, banging against the other bell. The raft dipped and rocked back and forth several times, levelled out and then stayed afloat. Everyone cried out in victory.

The long poles had floated away with the crash, so Ba directed Tangtun and two trackers to move into formation to swim beside the raft while he pointed it upstream.

"Keep it close to the bank so we can move faster," he said to the trackers on the bank with ropes.

"Let's go," Ba said.

Tangtun picked up speed with each stroke. We have to make it, we have to make it.

Ahead of them, they saw all the Jingnan villagers in wedding dress, crowded along the water's edge. The fishing boats and the first raft were docked and men were off-loading the other bells. The sight gave them new energy and they swam harder.

When Tangtun, Ba and the trackers nudged their raft into the bank, Little Ming and his father pulled it close and tied it. Other hands reached down to help lift father and son out of the stream. With water pouring off them, they straightened up to see soldiers pushing through the crowd.

"Jianjun, you missed the wedding," said the captain in a commanding voice. "Now you answer to the king!"

CHAPTER 41

Dragged dripping along the path behind his father, Tangtun's eyes darted right and left looking for help. Stunned villagers stood frozen. Then, he saw the Master Musician in the crowd holding two swords. With a mighty lunge, Tangtun grabbed his sword with both hands and started swinging at the soldiers. Yelling, they ducked and dodged and pulled out their own weapons.

Tangtun used the sword like an axe, hacking a spear handle in two and knocking another loose. He swiped at a guard's arm and blood spurted. Then a blow on top of his head made him lose his grip and his knees buckle. He heard his sword thud on the ground as his whole world turned black.

"Halt!" the captain shouted as Ba jumped back toward Tangtun. Other soldiers pulled him up short.

Little Ming and the Master Musician knelt beside Tangtun as he groaned and tried to sit up, holding his head. "What happened?" Tangtun said.

"You're fine. Can you stand up now?" asked the Master.

Stumbling to his feet, Tangtun saw that his sword was gone and BaBa was still captive. He whispered to them, "Get the big bells inside."

"But …" said Little Ming.

As two soldiers yanked him forward, he slung words over his shoulder, "Don't let anyone stop you, no matter what happens!"

Trying to stay on his feet, his mind jumped from one crazy idea to the next, but the soldiers gripped his arms tight. He tried to catch BaBa's eye, but he couldn't.

When they entered the city, growing numbers of curious people followed them along the street. At the palace steps, guards held the throngs back, while the soldiers pulled them up the steps to the great banquet hall and pushed through the crowd.

"Make way!" they ordered.

With his whole body on full alert, Tangtun took in the room. The fragrances of roast duck, steaming hot soup, and sweet rice wine filled his nostrils. Long silk gowns with diagonal stripes swished as women turned toward the door. Soft, stringed music and the low voices of drums and chime stones faded into silence behind staring men in braids. The spring green and yellow walls reflected myriad oil lights. The festive scene grated on Tangtun's nerves. Even the rack with two upper rows of bells set up by the road team seemed to sneer at him like a toothless old man.

King Wang rose from his seat centred behind the great banquet table on the raised platform.

"Kowtow!" ordered the guards, whacking Tangtun and BaBa across their backs.

Tangtun dropped to his knees and knocked his forehead on the floor. Out of the corner of his eye, he saw BaBa in the same position, but then BaBa began to stand.

Tangtun's pride lifted him up to stand beside his father.

"Jianjun? You finally show yourself before me? Today your treachery ends," bellowed the king.

Just then Tangtun saw Zigong seated at the table of honour near the bride and groom. Remembering his story about the way of fathers and sons, Tangtun sprang forward to speak.

The king stuck up his hand. "Do not speak." He continued with his voice rising with every word. "Before you were born, my father accepted your father into our family. We spent summers together as boys and grew up proud to be soldiers, guarding our king." Then, he shouted. "But, in the Battle of Ying, your father abandoned my father. Friends do not desert friends in time of need."

"But, he…" Tangtun tried again.

"Quiet!" the king thundered.

"Later my father and his real friend, the ruler of Zeng, returned to remove the enemies from our city. By then he was old and forgiving." Looking from Tangtun to Ba, the king sneered, "He let you live, Jianjun!"

Ba bowed his head silently.

"Do something, BaBa," said Tangtun gripping his father's arm.

Ba put a hand over Tangtun's and squeezed. "Be patient." Tangtun wasn't sure he had spoken.

"When I wanted my father to kill you, you worthless traitor, he only banished you from his sight," the king spluttered with fury as he paced up and down.

"But, then, this son of yours," the king turned and flicked his hand in Tangtun's direction, "this Tangtun, said you two could make the best wedding gift ever. I relented. I hoped this time, maybe this time you might be an honourable man, but no!"

He stomped his feet and shouted. "Again, you failed your king! Out, out of my sight!" He waved an arm at the soldiers. "Imprison those two. I will personally see to their deaths after the celebration ends!"

CHAPTER 42

Tangtun jerked his arms trying to get free from the soldiers dragging him out of the room. The soldiers slammed him upright against the wall. He couldn't even turn his head.

Ba whipped away from his guards with one of their swords in his hand. He lunged at a second one, disarming him before any of them could react, and pivoted toward another. Out of the corner of his eye, Tangtun could see the soldiers circling to trap Ba. Twisting hard, Tangtun broke free just as Ba's sword flew through the air. A soldier pierced Ba's side with his blade and Ba fell on his back with his head bouncing.

Tangtun screamed, "BaBa!" and ran toward him sliding to a stop on his knees and staring at the blood staining Ba's tunic. Cold fear froze Tangtun's body, stole his breath, and brought tears to his eyes. "No! You can't die, BaBa! Wake up!" He shook Ba's shoulder and got no response. A burst of hot fury jarred Tangtun back on his feet and one hand like a racer. He darted toward Ba's sword and grabbed the handle. As he rounded at a soldier, a heart-stopping deep sound rumbled through the room.

Bong! Bong! Bong!

Tangtun—and everyone else—turned to see what made the noise. The Master Musician again struck the Great Bell, their contest winner, with a long pole. Bong!

With the sound dying away, village men in twos and threes marched in with the heaviest bells and suspended them on hangers across the bottom row of the rack. Players in red dresses moved into place with their hammers and sticks. Thousands of gold characters sparkled from the shiny red and black lacquered rack and bells.

Just then Ba groaned, "Oh-oh-h."

Tangtun slumped to his knees. "You're alive!"

"I'm fine," said Ba, holding his bleeding side as soldiers pulled him to his feet.

Tangtun looked around as the crowd oohed and aahed. With a surge of joy, he rose up and swung his free, open hand in the direction of the bells. He announced in a loud voice, "Behold, the royal wedding gift!"

He nodded at the Master and a fanfare of sound began to fill the room. With a commanding glare at the soldiers to keep Tangtun and Ba pinned in their places, King Wang settled into his seat.

As the fanfare died away, one large bell and one small bell began ringing at the same time with a slight sound, a mere flutter. Other pairs of large and small bells joined one after the other until they all danced in matched steps. Next a single tiny bell joined each pair, until all the small bells rang like running children above the deeper duet. The pleasing sound made everyone smile.

Seated between King Wang and Marquis Yi, the bride and groom looked the picture of approving unity. She leaned forward in a creamy silk dress embroidered with a brown and olive phoenix carrying a flowering branch in its mouth and spreading its wings and feet in landing. Its tail intersected a branch carried by another phoenix beneath it. The groom crossed his arms across his red gauze tunic featuring a black and yellow striped tiger facing a khaki dragon.

The king sat immobile with his eyes fixed on the bells, so Tangtun had trouble reading his face. On the other hand, Marquis Yi was smiling, tapping his fingers on the chair arm, and swaying with the music.

The family of bells grew louder and louder, pairs of sound phrases rising and falling, celebrating the togetherness of the royal pair. Finally, the wedding song danced in a fast flourish to its end. Then the smiling chatter of the people increased until Tangtun wondered if it would ever stop. When it did, he held his breath.

"Well," King Wang harrumphed. "Well," he repeated and shifted in his chair.

"Well, indeed," Marquis Zeng Hou Yi, brother of the bride, stood with beaming face and exclaimed. "Of all the instruments I have collected, none is as great as these bells. No bells I've ever heard ring to the heavens the way these do. No bell set I've ever played is as large as this *bianzhong*. Well done, King Chu Hui Wang, son of my father's friend," and, he bowed very low toward the king.

The king stood to lift him up and smiled. "These bells are your bells, Marquis, a gift from the Great Kingdom of Chu to our loyal friend, the ruler of the Zeng people. May they forever ring our song of unity."

"Hail to the Heavenly Fang, giver of new life, for this remarkable gift." Yi bowed again and said, "And, may I humbly ask who created these bells?"

For a moment King Wang stood silent. Then he turned, motioned for Tangtun and Ba to step forward, and said, "These Chu artisans."

Tangtun and Ba moved toward the table and bowed their heads. The guards stayed close behind them. Taking a chance, Tangtun said, "And, the village of Jingnan!" Approving nods and ahs went round the room.

"Do you have another song?" King Wang asked Tangtun.

"The second song, Double Circle of Life, celebrates our two leaders and peoples in a musical union of metal and stone," replied Tangtun. He nodded to the Master again who strode across the room to the king's rack of chime stones.

Looking at the smallest bell player, Master struck a single small stone at the same time that she hit her tiny bell. The sounds teased everyone's ears. Other stones and bells began to war with each other, with the upper tier of bells seeming to chase the stones. The middle bells played a matched step, half-step melody while the large bells intertwined evenly spaced Ooo-OOH, Ooo, Ooo, Ooo underneath it all like Tangtun's doves. The warring sounds faded until only harmony remained. When the song ended, the king rose first, applauding enthusiastically. The wedding party and crowd joined him with cheers.

Marquis Yi bowed toward King Wang again and said, "I am a musician and I appreciate and praise such pure music. It heals and calms our spirits."

The king nodded and said, "Only the heavens could blend Chu music and Zeng music together in such harmony."

The marquis smiled. "King Wang, with this gift, our two peoples can remember Chu and Zeng as long as these marvelous bells ring."

Again hemmed in by two soldiers ready to kill him, Tangtun grunted a mirthless, "Ha!" and thought, *Forget all this music talk. We need an escape route.*

His eyes darted around the room searching for the best possibility. He hoped BaBa would follow his lead.

CHAPTER 43

"When music goes forth ..."

While King Wang and Marquis Yi bowed their heads in mutual admiration, Tangtun slammed his fists straight down out of the soldiers' grasp and lunged for the nearest door with BaBa on his heels. They made it out the door before the soldiers jerked them back into the room.

Tangtun glared at the king. "We delivered the best wedding gift anyone has ever created. I demand you release us!"

Ba put his hand on his arm, and said, "Stop, my son. It is useless."

Zigong rose beside the startled king and marquis with hands spread out flat.

With terse lips, King Wang said, "Speak, Master Zigong."

"Son of Heaven, our Master Teacher, Kongzi, taught us that when music goes forth, orderly relations are clear, the ears are sharp, the eyes bright, bringing life to a state of balance."

As the king nodded, Zigong continued, "By changing ways and customs, music brings peace to the entire world."

Yi smiled and said, "I agree, Master Zigong. Because of this marvelous wedding gift , our two peoples can continue to live as friends, and now as family, forever." Then he turned toward the king. "And in the family spirit, Son of Heaven, may I suggest that these two craft persons, who created this marvelous, musical gift, have pleased the Sky God? Will you also please him by sparing their lives?"

Tangtun breathed in sharply and exchanged looks with BaBa. King Wang wrinkled his brow, stroked his chin, and studied Marquis Yi for so long, Tangtun's whole body tensed up again.

Then the king spoke, "And so you may, for their incredible musical gift touched my ears, travelled to my heart, and then to my soul. The music restored my feelings for my former friend and also for his son."

Turning toward Tangtun and Ba, he nodded at the soldiers to release them. "You are correct in asking for your release, Tangtun. Heaven demands that I acknowledge the creators of such a musical instrument. You, Jianjun, did not fail your king this time. I declare you to be the Royal Artisan of the Chu from this day forward. And, the foundry of Jingnan Village is now the Royal Foundry of the Chu State!"

Ba bowed silently but Tangtun could see the corners of his mouth lift.

"And, in honour of both our fathers, I give the land my father seized from you, Jianjun, to your son. Keep it well, young Tangtun, for your children and your children's children."

Feeling light enough to float away, Tangtun bowed deeply also.

"May I speak?" asked Ba.

"You may."

Tangtun thought, *Careful, BaBa. He can still kill us.*

"Our fathers smile today, King Wang. They are happy our dispute ends, for *du li nan zhi*, one person alone is not strong enough. And, my gratitude to you is exceeded only by …" He paused, turned toward Tangtun and added, "my appreciation of my son."

Tangtun's view of the room receded until he could see only the face of his father.

"Our ancestors often said, *Lu yaozhi ma li, ri jiu jianrenxin.* Over a long distance, you learn the strength of your horse; over a long time, you learn the moral character of your friend. With this wisdom, our fathers praised anyone who remained true in difficulties."

He turned toward Tangtun. "Today I say it to honour your father, you King Wang, and my son. *Lu yaozhi ma li, ri jiu jianrenxin.*"

Tangtun bowed his entire body low again, this time toward his father. His smile stretched every muscle of his face and he felt happy to his toes. As he rose, he tipped his head in a salute to Zigong, acknowledging that fathers do protect sons, and sons, fathers. He thought, *I'm so glad I didn't become an army spy.*

The king clapped his hands, "Let the celebration continue!" Every musical instrument in the room began to play dance music.

MaMa bandaged BaBa's side while whispering to him. Tangtun didn't need to hear her. He knew she was telling BaBa the same thing she had just said to him. Her scolding, "Foolish one, you could have been killed," really meant, "I'm glad you are alive."

The party lasted late into the night. Everyone congratulated Tangtun, Ba, and the villagers. Master Musician and Zigong strolled past Tangtun. "Your father and you have done well," said the Master Musician, "proving once again *du li nan zhi*, one alone is not strong enough."

"You flatter me," said Tangtun keeping his face still, while delight shimmered deep inside.

"You are an upright young man," added Zigong, walking on with a smile.

Meimei tugged on Tangtun's sleeve and said, "You're always Gege, Older Brother, to me."

Nainai hugged him. "Now you know all the mystery of your BaBa."

When it was time, father and son strode out together. The family climbed in the waggon along with Little Ming. Master Musician and Haohao sat with the driver.

Ba said to Tangtun, "I know you lost your knife in the river. When we get home, I will make you an even better one for carving animals."

Tangtun smiled and dipped his head in respect.

Ba reached down and picked up his sword, then handed it to Tangtun. "Today you fought bravely to protect me from the troubles I brought on us all. You are an upright son, so I also give you my sword."

Ba continued, "And in the presence of the family and our dear friends, and on this happy occasion, I announce a new name for you, my son. You are no longer Tangtun, but *Fuyi*, *Fu* because you give of yourself and *Yi* because your mind is filled with new ideas."

Speechless with gifts and, even more so, the sound of pride in his father's voice, Tangtun bowed his head again. Behind him, he heard Little Ming whisper, "Yes!" and Haohao respond with, "Aww."

Then they all looked up at the clear night sky. Millions of stars poured like a stream of milk across the heavens. The Great Bear's tail pointed toward the home of the morning sun, heralding spring and new life.

Tangtun said, "Next I, Fuyi, will paint this night sky."

***

ABOUT 25 YEARS LATER

Chu State, Jingnan Village

"*Ai-yah!*" Fuyi strained to control the chariot's lunging horses on the river road in front of the foundry. A huge bronze bell tipped half out of the swaying vehicle, saved at the last second by two men riding inside.

"Moving this bell may be as much trouble as the whole set of bells," Little Ming said, laughing and hanging on its bronze edge to set it back down.

The larger man jammed in a wooden beam to brace the bell and grunted, "And it may be the most important."

Fuyi nodded agreement with his lifelong friends. "With the first bell, I didn't know who to fear more, my father demanding I be a man like him or King Wang trying to kill us all."

“And now, the king demanded you make this bell for Marquis Yi’s funeral,” said Ming.

“The perfect send-off to a musical heaven,” Haohao said.

"Time to go," said Fuyi. “I see our escort coming.”

He clicked the horses forward to join the king’s guards, saying, “I'm more than ready to be done with this part of our lives.”

***

ABOUT A MONTH LATER AND 200 MILES NORTH

Zeng State, Suizhou City

Tomb of Marquis Yi

Swoosh. Thud! Pound, pound! Fuyi, Little Ming and Haohao watched men pack charcoal to close the entrance of the tomb of Marquis Yi of Zeng. They sealed inside with the music-loving ruler, the sixty-five bells and young women bell players, another five dozen instruments, his favourite dog, chariots, horses, weapons, and other treasured items.

Ming said, “I hope the marquis sings and dances to these bells forever in his ancestral home.”

As the three old friends turned down the hillside toward the sunny valley below, Fuyi added, “For sure, no living person will ever hear our bells played again.”

And no one did—

Until—once again—

Scrape, scrape. Swoosh. Thud! Swoosh. Thud ....

***

ALMOST 2500 YEARS LATER

Suizhou City, Hubei Province, People's Republic of China

Tomb of Marquis Yi

1977 CE

As hordes of people came and went, the tomb of Marquis Yi disappeared under almost forty feet of soil. The use of bronzeware and two-toned bells disappeared from Chinese culture. Then, in 1977, men clearing land for an army training-camp in Suizhou, Hubei Province, rediscovered the tomb and its contents, including the bell set, intact and playable.

THE TIME OF TANGTUN

Near the end of China's Spring-Autumn Period (770-ca. 475 BCE)

And the beginning of the Warring States Period (ca. 475-221 BCE)

In the chronology below, fictional people, dates, and events are italicized.

490 BCE Battle of Ying—the Chu capital city falls. King Zhao escapes to the protection of the Zeng State ruler, probably the father of Marquis Yi.

489 BCE King Zhao reclaims Ying

488 BCE King Zhao dies. Prince Wang becomes King Wang, ruler of the Chu.

457 BCE King Wang adds the Zeng State to the Chu kingdom.

456 BCE *Tangtun is twelve years old. Battle of the Chu Artisans*

455 BCE *Royal Chu wedding happens in the spring at Fang Festival time.*

433 BCE Marquis Yi, owner of the bell set, dies at the age of forty-five.

King Wang orders a funerary bell as a memorial gift.

Tangtun, now thirty-five years old, makes the special bell and watches it being buried with Marquis Yi and his entire set of bells.

432 BCE King Wang dies after a fifty-six-year rule. (His posthumous title is King Hui of Chu.)

THE BELLS TODAY

Bianzhong, the Bells of Marquis Yi of Zeng, or the *Zenghouyi* Bells, hang today behind glass in the Provincial Museum of Hubei in Wuhan, China. The main hall contains the permanent exhibition of artifacts of Yi's tomb—an additional sixty musical instruments, lacquered ware, bamboo slips covered with bronze-age script telling the story of the funeral procession and ceremony, gold and jade items, and more than 22,000 pounds of ancient and intricate pieces of bronze work. It is noteworthy that many items have written on them, "for the use of Marquis Yi," implying a shift from pleasing ancestors to pleasing the individual. The museum also includes a concert hall where a replica set of the bells is played daily. A third building holds exhibits informing visitors about the Chu people.

Many Chinese and Western scholars have studied, and continue to study, the bells of this ancient tomb. A few early ones include Tan Weisi, author of *Zeng Hou Yi Tomb* (Wenhu Press, 2001); Wang Hongxing, Curator of Hubei Provincial Museum; Huang Xiangpeng of China's Central Academy of Music; Robert Bagley of Princeton University, professor of Chinese art history and a specialist in pre-Han art and archaeology; and Lothar von Falkenhausen, Professor of Chinese Archaeology and Art History and author of *Suspended Music: Chime-Bells in the Culture of Bronze Age China* (University of Los Angeles Press, 1993).

Bagley says, "In the archaeology of ancient music this discovery ['the buried orchestra'] is the most important one ever made anywhere in the world." Von Falkenhausen calls the bells the "Rosetta Stone for the study of ancient Chinese music."

As important as the bells are for history, metallurgy, musicology, cosmology, and culture, no one knows for certain why they were made. They were probably used for important ceremonies. This story of Tangtun and his father provides an imaginary reason for the making of the bell set and also imagines the identity of the makers of the funerary bell, the final bell.

Irene Vinyard Bennett at a replica set of the Bells of Marquis Yi, Chinese University of Hong Kong Music Archives, 7 September 2012. Photo by Phillip N Bennett.

FACTS ABOUT THE BELL SET

- The bells of Marquis Yi weigh almost 6,000 pounds (2.75 tons USA) and the racks weigh almost 10,000 pounds (4.8 tons USA) making them the largest musical instrument in the world.
- They are the only complete set of *bianzhong* or ceremonial chime bells found intact and still playable.
- The inscription on the funerary bell, the 56th year of the reign of King Wang of Chu, means the bell set itself was made before 433 BCE.
- The inscription also reveals that the final bell was a gift of the Chu ruler when Marquis Yi died. To show respect, the Zeng moved the large bells to make room on the rack for hanging the Chu funerary gift bell.
- Some bells play the chromatic scale, like today's pianos, predating the final Western development of the chromatic scale in medieval Europe by about one thousand years.
- No one knows for certain how foundry workers were able to tune each bell to play two tones and cast the name of the tone into the bell before it was made, but their acoustical properties are scientifically sophisticated.
- The grave flooded with water shortly after it was sealed, preserving almost everything in it. Scientists researched how to remove water-logged, lacquered wooden items, especially the bell rack, so the wood did not dry out quickly and disintegrate in the air.

- The bells and rack contain 3755 Chinese characters recording the music notation of five regions of China, including the Chu and the Zeng.
- No modern-day metallurgist has been able to replicate the exact bronze formula of the bell material, but a credible duplicate has been made.
- No 5th-century BCE musical score exists for the bells, but modern-day musicians are writing music for them—alone, with ancient Chinese instruments, and with modern Chinese and Western instruments.
- A reproduced set of bells tour the world with millions having heard them in concert. Now they are played almost daily at the Hubei Provincial Museum, Wuchang District, Wuhan, Hubei Province, China.
- The original *Zenghouyi* Bells have been played in China only three times. On China's Army Day, 1 August 1978, a group of musicians and archaeologists played the bells for the first time in 2,411 years. In 1984, at the 35th Anniversary of new China in Beijing, foreign diplomats and government officials heard them in concert. On 1 July 1997 in Hong Kong, the Imperial Bells Ensemble of China played them as part of the state ceremony reuniting Hong Kong with China. That commissioned work, *Symphony 1997*, featured Tan Dun (China's premier composer and conductor), the Hong Kong Philharmonic Orchestra, Yo-Yo Ma (Cellist), and Yip's Children's Choir.
- And in September 2013, for the first time, a full replica set of the *bianzhong* of Marquis Yi of Zeng, a Chinese orchestra, and a

Western organ performed together in the Hong Kong Cultural Center in Tsim Sha Tsui, Kowloon. They played music written especially for that momentous, first ever East meets West concert.

May the bells of Marquis Yi ring on forever, encouraging world peace and harmony!

AUTHOR'S NOTE

I first learned of Marquis Yi's bell set when I saw a book in the Arts and Culture section of the Hong Kong Central Library entitled *Suspended Music*, one of the earliest books written about them. One sentence surprised me, *"No one knows why these bells were made."* I immediately thought, *I do,* as Tangtun, a figment of my imagination, sprang into my mind. The result is this novel, but many people, places and events of the story were real.

DaJiang River is today's Yangtze River.

King Zhao, King Wang, and Marquis Yi were real men who lived in and ruled the Chu and Zeng regions in 5th-century BCE, pre-united, ancient China. Zigong (formal name, Duanmu Ci, 520-456 BCE), travelled with Kongzi, whose Western name is Confucius, to the state of Chu. He could have re-visited there at the time of Tangtun.

Chinese scholars have debated the meaning of Confucius' *Upright Man* story for 2500 years with most seeing it as a statement about the relationship between society and government. I chose to use the earliest version of the story, before the academic debate started, to be only a Confucian statement about father-son relationships.

Early Chinese books credit an inventor who lived near the time of Confucius (c 551 – c 479 BCE) with making the wooden spy kite, so its reference here is timely.

The Chinese invented the *Hand Command* game, or *Centipede-Frog-Snake*, about the time of this story. Today many versions exist globally under different names. The Western version is known as *Rock-Paper-Scissors*.

Elephants and rhinoceroses existed on the plains of central China at the time of this story. Rhinoceros skin became tough leather armour for soldiers and their horses, and elephants' tails were reportedly torched in the Boju battle.

The fictional Battle of Ying in Tangtun's story is based on the real Battle of Boju (506 BCE) but the story battle happens later. The Chu king at the time, King Zhao, escaped to the Zeng area when the Chu capital city fell to the enemy. The Zeng ruler welcomed him, and later Zhao's friends helped Zhao recapture the city. His son, Wang, succeeded him as the Chu king.

The star formation, the Great Bear, has been called many names across time—plough, waggon, canoe, hunters hunting bear, etc. Westerners call it the Big Dipper or Ursa Major. In 5th-century BCE China, the Chu people could see the Great Bear changing position year-round and therefore easily identified seasons. Also, the Chu people made sacrifices to the springtime constellation Fang, hoping for good weather for planting and crops, but the Fang Festival Day in this story is imaginary.

When Marquis Yi, ruler of the Zeng, died in 433 BCE, seventy-three years after the Battle of Boju, the Chu son sent the funerary bell as a memorial gift. To show respect, the lower bells on the already existing set of bells were moved to allow for the hanging of the memorial gift bell.

No one knows how long it took to make the Yi bell set, but it probably took longer than the single year this story covers. Scholars debate whether the bells were made by the Chu or Zeng, but for this story, they are made in the Chu State.

For the sake of a good story, I exercised literary license to compress time and events and to credit Tangtun with the work of many other real but unknown bronze artists. And I made his Jingnan Village foundry a private bronze business seeking royal patronage. In reality, no 5th century foundry was private in the modern sense, for they all probably required funding from rich benefactors.

For four or five centuries before Tangtun's story, Chinese metalworkers had already cast characters in metal and begun to do gold inlay. Also, several bell sets, one with 26 bells from 6th century BCE, have been excavated, so the Yi bells are the magnificent end-product of years of experimenting with music and metal. In this story, Tangtun the artist first thinks of casting characters in metal and lining them with gold in the largest chime bell set ever.

Also, iron was discovered in northern China in the third millennium BCE. Several centuries before this story, a few areas were producing cast iron, though innovation happened at different rates in different places. Near Tangtun's time, the Chu State led in iron production, but no iron objects were found in the tomb of Marquis Yi. Additionally, the Chu-made funerary bell matched the bronze set, while the Houma foundry in the area of modern-day Wuhan, made bronze, not iron, from the 6th to

2nd centuries BCE. The terra cotta soldiers made 200 years before the Yi bells carry bronze weapons, not iron swords. These facts support the idea that bronze and iron work co-existed for several centuries, making the end of the Chinese Bronze Age hard to pinpoint. Hence, for this story, iron is a threat to Tangtun's village foundry.

ADVANCE COMMENTS

From Merrill J. Davies

Irene Bennett's novel, *Battle of the Artisans*, is an unusual and compelling story worthy of recognition. It is well-researched, and Bennett gives the reader just enough background details to be able to empathize with twelve-year-old Tangtun's conflicts in 5th Century BCE China, but not enough to be boring. Strong themes of the importance of working together in community and typical father-son conflicts add to the value of the novel, as well as help the reader see the progress of both Tangtun and Ba, his father, as they struggle to live together peacefully. Musicians and artists of all ages will especially enjoy this well-written story.

Merrill J. Davies, Ed. Specialist
Retired High School English Teacher
Author, *The Welsh Harp* (2012), *Becoming Jestina* (2018), *Tulsa Times* (2023)

From Aziz D. Barnard Luce

Battle of the Artisans: Making the Bells of Marquis Yi is a fast-paced novel about the making of a Chinese national treasure from the Warring States period. Themes such as parents' duty to their children, a child's desire for parental approval, and the importance of community while navigating a changing world are balanced with enjoyable details of ancient China, including mega-fauna of the region as well as familiar children's games. For the music lover, Bennett's treatment of music and its possibilities weaves the varied themes of the novel into a single harmonious tale.

It is fitting that the unsung heroes of the musical world—the instrument makers—are the protagonists of this tale about the origins of one of the greatest musical instruments to survive from antiquity.

Aziz D. Barnard Luce, Principal percussionist,
Hong Kong Symphony Orchestra

From Janet Mann

Good storytelling can bring history alive, and *Battle of the Artisans* is good storytelling.

The origin of the bells of Marquis Yi has puzzled historians since they were first discovered. Here Irene Bennett has created a world where the possibility of making this amazing musical instrument might have been envisaged. Through the story of a young boy, Tangtun, she leads us through a period of history where so much was achieved but not recorded. Tangtun's growing maturity mirrors the development of the great bells, and their completion marks the blossoming of a truly mature relationship with his father.

A thoughtful and thought-provoking read for all ages.

Janet Mann, Librarian
Author, *The School Library Book – a guide to effective school libraries* (Scholastic Asia 2021)

THE PUBLISHERS

Proverse Hong Kong (PVHK), founded by Gillian and Verner Bickley, is based in Hong Kong with long-term and developing regional and international connections.

Proverse has published (mainly literary) fiction (novels, novellas, single author short-story collections), non-fiction (including autobiography and biography, history, letters, memoirs, sport, travel narratives contemporary and archival), single-author poetry collections, children's, young adult, and academic books. Other interests include academic works in the humanities, social sciences, cultural studies, linguistics and education. Some Proverse books have accompanying audio texts. Some are translated from or into Chinese or other languages.

We welcome authors who have a story to tell, wisdom, perceptions or information to convey, a person they want to memorialize, a neglect they want to remedy, a record they want to correct, a strong interest that they want to share, skills they want to teach, and who consciously seek to make a contribution to society in an informative, interesting and well-written way. Proverse works with texts by non-native-speaker writers of English as well as by native English-speaking writers.

The name, "Proverse", combines the words "prose" and "verse" and is pronounced accordingly.

THE INTERNATIONAL PROVERSE PRIZE FOR UNPUBLISHED BOOK-LENGTH FICTION, NON-FICTION OR POETRY

The Proverse Prize, an annual international competition for an unpublished single-author book-length work of fiction, non-fiction, or poetry, the original work of the entrant, submitted in English (unpublished translations welcomed) was established in January 2008. It is open to all who are at least eighteen on the date they sign the entry form and without restriction of nationality, residence or citizenship.

Founded by Gillian and Verner Bickley, the objectives of the prize are: to encourage excellence and / or excellence and usefulness in publishable written work in the English Language, which can, in varying degrees, "delight and instruct". Entries are invited from anywhere in the world.

The Prize

1) Publication by Proverse Hong Kong, with
2) Cash prize of HKD10,000 (HKD7.80 = approx. USD1.00)

Extent of the Manuscript: within the range of what is usual from time to time for the genre of the work submitted. However, it is advisable that novellas be in the range, 30,000 to 45,000 words; other fiction (e.g. novels, short-story collections) and non-fiction (e.g. autobiographies, biographies, diaries, letters, memoirs, essay collections, etc.) should be in the range, 75,000 to 100,000 words. Poetry collections could be in the range, 3,000 to 5,000 words and single long poems could be a maximum of 25,000 words. Other word-counts and mixed-genre submissions are not ruled out.

THE INTERNATIONAL PROVERSE POETRY PRIZE (SINGLE POEMS)

An annual international Proverse Poetry Prize (for single poems) was established in 2016. The international Proverse Poetry Prize is open to all who are at least eighteen years old whatever their residence, nationality or citizenship.

Single poems, submitted in English, are invited on (a) any subject or theme, chosen by the writer OR (b) on a subject or theme selected by the organizers.

Poems may be in any form, style or genre. Each poem should be no more than 30 lines.

Entries should previously be unpublished in any way (except in the case of unpublished translations into English of the entrant's own work already published in another language, providing the entrant holds the copyright).

If there are enough good entries in any year, an anthology of prize-winners and selected other entries will be published.

Judging usually takes place at the same time as the judging for the Proverse Prize for unpublished book-length fiction, non-fiction or poetry.

Judges: anonymous (as for the Proverse Prize for an unpublished book-length work).

Max number of entries per person: No maximum.

No poet may win more than one prize in any one year.

The above information is for guidance only.
More information, updated from time to time, is available at the Proverse website: proversepublishing.com

International Proverse Prize and International Proverse Poetry Prize (Single Poems) Annual Entry Deadlines
(subject to confirmation and/or change)

Entry Forms, Terms and Conditions updated for the current year on the Proverse Hong Kong website. Before this, reference to the previous year's information provides good guidance.	No later than 14 April
Receipt of Entry Fees, Entry Forms, Entered work begins.	7 May
Deadline for receipt of Entry Fees, Entry Forms, Entered work.	30 June
Period for receipt of late entries (Entry Fees, Entry Forms, Entered work). Please NB, an increased entry fee is payable for late entries.	1 July – 15 July

The above information is for guidance only.
More information, updated from time to time, is available at the Proverse website: proversepublishing.com

FICTION PUBLISHED BY PROVERSE HONG KONG

NOVELS

A Misted Mirror. Gillian Jones.
A Painted Moment. Jennifer Ching.
Adam's Franchise. Lawrence Gray.
An Imitation of Life. Laura Solomon.
Article 109. Peter Gregoire.
As Leaves Blow. Philip Chatting.
Bao Bao's Odyssey: From Mao's Shanghai to Capitalist Hong Kong. Paul Ting.
Black Tortoise Winter. Jan Pearson.
Blue Dragon Spring. Jan Pearson.
Bright Lights and White Lights. Andrew Carter.
Cemetery miss you. Jason S Polley.
Cop Show Heaven. Lawrence Gray.
Cry of the Flying Rhino. Ivy Ngeow.
Curveball: Life Never Comes At You Straight. Gustav Preller.
Death Has A Thousand Doors. Patricia W. Grey.
Enoch's Muse. Sergio Monteiro.
Finley's Confession. George Watt.
Hilary and David. Laura Solomon.
HK Hollow. Dragoş Ilca.
Hong Kong Rocks. Peter Humphreys.
Instant Messages. Laura Solomon.
Jane, Frank and Mia. Dami Jung.
Man's Last Song. James Tam.
Mishpacha—Family. Rebecca Tomasis.
Paranoia. Caleb Kavon.
Professor Everywhere. Nicholas Binge.
Red Bird Summer. Jan Pearson.
Revenge from Beyond. Dennis Wong.
The Day They Came. Gerard Breissan.
The Devil You Know. Peter Gregoire.
The Handover Murders. Damon Rose.
The Monkey in Me. Caleb Kavon.
The Perilous Passage of Princess Petunia Peasant. Victor Edward Apps.
The Reluctant Terrorist. Caleb Kavon.

The Thing Is. Andrew Carter.
The Village in the Mountains. David Diskin.
Three Wishes in Bardo. Feng Chi-shun.
Tiger Autumn. Jan Pearson.
Tightrope! A Bohemian Tale. Olga Walló. (Translated from Czech.)
Tree Crime, Melody Kemp.
University Days. Laura Solomon.
Vera Magpie. Laura Solomon. (Novella.)

SHORT STORY COLLECTIONS

Beyond Brightness. Sanja Särman.
Odds and Sods. Lawrence Gray.
The Shingle Bar Sea Monster and Other Stories. Laura Solomon.
The Snow Bridge And Other Stories. Philip Chatting.
Under the shade of the Feijoa trees and other stories. Hayley Ann Solomon.

FIND OUT MORE ABOUT PROVERSE AUTHORS, BOOKS, EVENTS AND LITERARY PRIZES

Visit our website: <https://www.proversepublishing.com>
Visit the Proverse page on our Hong Kong distributor's website:
<https://cup.cuhk.edu.hk/Proversehk>
Follow us on Twitter / X: twitter.com/Proversebooks
"Like" us on www.facebook.com/ProversePress

Request our free E-Newsletter
Send your request to <info@proversepublishing.com>.

Availability
Most Proverse titles
are available in Hong Kong and world-wide
from our Hong Kong based distributor,
the Chinese University of Hong Kong Press,
The Chinese University of Hong Kong, Shatin, NT,
Hong Kong SAR, China.

Most titles can be ordered online from amazon
(various countries) and other online retailers.

Stock-holding retailers
Hong Kong (CUHKP, Bookazine)
Canada (Elizabeth Campbell Books),
Andorra (Llibreria La Puça, La Llibreria).
UK (Ivybridge Bookshop, Devon).

Orders may be made from bookshops
in the UK and elsewhere.

Ebooks and audiobooks
Most of our titles are available also as Ebooks and increasingly as audiobooks.

Made in the USA
Columbia, SC
09 June 2025

59065535R00120